She wanted to feel safe.

Her lips parted. Her eyelids closed. *Kiss me, Jake.* Breathless, she waited.

The pressure of his mouth against hers was firm and sweet. They shared a breath, an incredible intimacy. Excitement bubbled up inside her. She trembled, aware that this might be the best kiss she'd ever had in her entire life, not wanting this moment to end.

Too soon, he withdrew. Her eyes opened and met his. Both of them knew that kissing was inappropriate.

She hadn't intended to put him in this position, but when he'd spoken so candidly of his father, she'd been touched. Jake wasn't a man who shared his emotions. The lone wolf. He didn't involve anyone else in his problems.

But he'd told her. For some reason, he'd trusted her.

"Tomorrow morning," he said.

"I'll be ready at eight o'clock."

She took a backward step as he left the room and closed the door. She and Jake were going to make a very good team.

USA TODAY Bestselling Author

CASSIE MILES

SOVEREIGN SHERIFF

TORONTO NEW YORK LONDON
AMSTERDAM PARIS SYDNEY HAMBURG
STOCKHOLM ATHENS TOKYO MILAN MADRID
PRAGUE WARSAW BUDAPEST AUCKLAND

In memory of Martha Pogrew and her red stiletto heels.

Special thanks and acknowledgment to Cassie Miles for her contribution to the Cowboys Royale series.

Recycling programs for this product may not exist in your area.

ISBN-13: 978-0-373-69560-7

SOVEREIGN SHERIFF

Copyright © 2011 by Harlequin Books S.A.

ABOUT THE AUTHOR

Though born in Chicago and raised in L.A., Cassie Miles has lived in Colorado long enough to be considered a semi-native. The first home she owned was a log cabin in the mountains overlooking Elk Creek, with a thirty-mile commute to her work at the *Denver Post*.

After raising two daughters and cooking tons of macaroni and cheese for her family, Cassie is trying to be more adventurous in her culinary efforts. Seviche, anyone? She's discovered that almost anything tastes better with wine. When she's not plotting Harlequin Intrigue books, Cassie likes to hang out at the Denver Botanical Gardens near her high-rise home.

Books by Cassie Miles

CAST OF CHARACTERS

Jake Wolf—The recently elected sheriff of Wind River County battles corruption in his department, prejudice against his Native American heritage and complications from crimes against the visiting royals.

Saida Khalid—The fashionista princess of Jamala attends law school in California. Drawn into royal intrigues, she trusts no one but the sheriff to find her missing brother.

Sheik Amir Khalid—The black sheep ruler of Jamala is missing and feared dead.

Maggie Wolf—Jake's younger sister studies psychology at University of Wyoming and wants her brother to find a mate.

Danny Harold—The paparazzo who specializes in photos of royals has a secret agenda when it comes to Princess Saida.

Sheik Efraim Aziz—His old-fashioned ideas and imperious manner are softened by his love for an American woman.

Callie McGuire—As the assistant to the Secretary of Foreign Affairs, she is based in D.C., but her roots are in Wyoming.

Burt Maddox—Though the blustering former sheriff was suspected of corruption, he thinks he should run this county.

Wade Freeman—A local rancher looking into the oil business has a mysterious connection to Saida's missing brother.

Prince Sebastian and Prince Antoine Cavanaugh—The twin brothers are corulers of the island nation of Barajas.

Prince Stefan Lutece—Ruler of Kyros.

Jane Cameron—The plain-Jane forensics expert for Wind River County has been glowing since she met Stefan.

Prince Darek Ramat—The Prince of Saruk would like to take over the interests of COIN.

Chapter One

A night breeze swept down from the peaks of the Wind River Mountains and cooled the high Wyoming prairie. At his home five miles outside Dumont, Sheriff Jake Wolf opened his arms wide and welcomed the wind against his bare chest. His arms stretched over his head for a couple of modified jumping jacks. His twelve-hour workday was over. Thankfully, there had been no major catastrophes. No sniper attacks. No bomb explosions. No murderous abductions.

After he adjusted his jeans on his hips, he picked up a basketball and began to dribble slowly. The smack of the ball against concrete reminded him of his glory days at the Wyoming Indian High School when the Chiefs had won their first state tournament. Basketball meant more to him than the powwow drumming and the traditions of his Arapaho people. The first thing he did when he'd bought this two-story, cedar-frame house was mount a hoop and backboard above the garage doors. Earlier this summer, he'd hung a couple of floodlights so he could play after dark.

He made a quick pivot in his sneakers, dodging an invisible foe and went in for a layup. Swish through the net. Two points. He backed up, dribbled, aimed a hook shot. Another score. The physical exertion felt great. He ran and shot, ran and shot. Sometimes a hit, sometimes a miss. He wanted to sweat, to get his blood pumping, to feel alive. All day long he'd been clenching his fists, holding on to his self-control while he fended off reporters, coordinated with other law enforcement agencies and investigated a series of crimes the likes of which Wind River County had never seen. It all started a few weeks ago when the princes and sheiks of four island nations in the Mediterranean arrived for a summit meeting at the exclusive Wind River Ranch and Resort. The trouble wasn't over yet; Sheik Amir Khalid was still missing.

Jake ran back for a three-pointer, turned and shot. The ball dropped neatly through the hoop. *Nothing but net, baby.*

"And the crowd goes wild." His sister, Maggie, strolled from the two-story cedar house. "Come inside and eat. I made a recipe from the Food Network. Linguini with meatballs."

"Not hungry." With the way his sister cooked, he expected the meatballs to be the consistency of petrified elk droppings.

"Come on, Jake. You're in decent shape for an old man of thirty-one, but you need to watch it. You're going to get too skinny and no woman will have you."

"Says the worldly nineteen-year-old."

"Seriously." She knocked the ball from his hand and shoved a bottle of water at him. "I'm only here for the summer. Who's going to take care of you when I'm back in college?"

"I'll manage." Before the royals came to town, his time had been structured and sane. Usually, he'd come home for a lunch break when he tended to the three horses in the barn behind the house.

"It's not like you have a social life," Maggie said. "In the time I've been here, you haven't gone on one single date."

True enough. He'd been elected sheriff less than a year ago and was still preoccupied with cleaning up the mess left behind by Big Burt Maddox, the former sheriff. He uncapped his water bottle and took a drink. "Too busy."

"The whole family is worried about you."

He had two other younger sisters. One was married. The other had a steady job in Denver. Mama still lived on the rez. When all four of these women got together, they were a force to be reckoned with. "I'm fine."

She dribbled toward the basket and made a layup. Her cutoffs and baggy T-shirt didn't match her weird curlicue hairdo—no doubt a style she'd picked up from some fashion program on cable. Signing up for satellite television with over two hundred channels had been a mistake; his sister was starting to quote supermodels.

She flipped the basketball back to him and said, "There's a name for what's wrong with you. The lone wolf syndrome. Just like that stupid belt buckle you always wear."

He touched his lucky pewter belt buckle with the howling wolf design. "What's wrong with this?"

"If you'd sit down for a minute, I could explain. Lucky for you, I'm majoring in psychology."

He looked toward the road and saw headlights turning off the road into his driveway. Gravel crunched under the wheels of a dark green sedan that pulled up and parked in front of his porch. A glance at his wristwatch told him that it was nine-forty-seven, which was too late for a friendly visit. *Now what?*

A slender woman with shining black hair emerged from the driver's side. Her jacket was metallic gold, and her jeans fit like a second skin. Balanced on sandals with high platform heels, she came toward them. "Are you the sheriff? Jake Wolf?"

He nodded. "Who are you?"

She stepped onto the concrete, straightened her shoulders and announced, "I am Princess Saida Khalid of Jamala."

Inwardly, he groaned. *Not another royal!*

His sister approached the princess and attempted a curtsy

that looked ridiculous in sneakers and cutoffs. "I'm Maggie, Jake's sister. Love your jacket. Is it designer?"

"Don't remember." She shrugged. "I've had it so long, it's practically vintage."

Maggie laughed as though this comment was the cleverest thing she'd ever heard. "Please come inside, Princess. Is that right? Should I call you Princess or Your Highness?"

"Call me Saida."

"Did you come here from Jamala?" Maggie frowned. "Is that far? I don't know exactly where Jamala is."

"An island nation in the Mediterranean. But I live in Beverly Hills."

Judging by Maggie's rapturous response, California was right next door to Heaven. She babbled about Hollywood and movie stars and some kind of shopping area called Rodeo Drive—a place that didn't sound as though they sold saddles and bridles. She tugged at her curled hair in an attempt to match Saida's smooth bangs and straight shoulder-length style.

Nothing good could come from his sister idolizing a princess. He grabbed his dark blue uniform shirt from the ground where he'd tossed it, stuck his arms in the sleeves and fastened two buttons. "What can I do for you, ma'am?"

Saida smiled at Maggie. "Will you excuse us, please?"

"Absolutely." His sister scampered toward the house. "You're coming in, right? I have linguini."

"I'll be right there," Jake said.

"I wasn't asking you."

He knew what Maggie meant, and she was going to be disappointed. He had no intention of encouraging the princess to stay.

"I adore linguini," Saida said, "with clam sauce."

"I've got to get your recipe." Maggie rolled her eyes. "What am I saying? You don't cook for yourself. I mean—"

"Maggie," Jake interrupted, "that's enough."

He was sick and tired of all this kowtowing to the royal entourage. As individuals, he'd come to respect the princes; they were decent men stuck in a bad situation. But he was more than ready for them to get the hell out of Wind River County.

As Maggie disappeared into the house, Saida strode across the basketball court toward him. She made direct eye contact, compelling him to meet her gaze. A striking woman with flawless olive skin and full lips, she was as pretty as the models in his sister's magazines. Looking into her caramel-colored eyes, he was surprised by the depth of sadness he saw there.

"You must help me." She grasped his arm, and he felt the trembling in her fingers. "Please. Help me find my brother."

Her pain was honest, not a facade. He could tell that her heart was aching, and her vulnerability touched him. He'd always been a sucker for the underdog; it was his nature to protect those who couldn't fend for themselves.

But he doubted that the princess fell under that category. She had too many advantages. Not only was she rich and royal but her beauty was an undeniable asset. All she needed to do was flutter those thick, black eyelashes and most men would jump to do her bidding.

Very deliberately, he removed her hand from his arm. "Amir went missing a while ago. Why are you coming here now?"

"Do you think I waited because I don't care about my brother?"

Or she was too busy getting a manicure. "Why now?"

"All my life, my brother has tried to shelter me. He's almost ten years older than I am. His friends—Sheik Efraim and the others—thought they were doing as Amir would wish

when they told me not to worry, that everything was fine."
Her amber eyes flashed. "They lied to me."

A harsh judgment. Even if the princes had deceived her,
news reporters and paparazzi had been all over this case.
"You must have seen the reports."

"The media." She flicked her hand as if swatting an irritating gnat. "I know better than to believe what I see on the
ten o'clock news. I thought I could trust my brother's friends.
But I've given up on them. They won't answer my questions.
The FBI agents refused to speak to me. I have come to you
to hear the truth."

"Lucky me," he muttered.

"I read about you on the internet. You promised change
when you ran for sheriff. You want to help people and fight
corruption. There were some amazing endorsements."

He eyed her skeptically. "If you've been in this country for
any time at all, you must know that you can't believe much
of what's said during a campaign."

"I've lived in America since I was sixteen."

That must be why she had only a slight accent, just a hint
of the exotic.

She continued, "It's true that politicians will say anything
to win. But you're different. I trust you."

He had a pretty good idea that she was shining him on to
get what she wanted. "You figured out that I'm trustworthy
by looking me up on the internet?"

Her full lips parted in a smile, showing off her perfect,
white teeth. When she leaned toward him, he caught a whiff
of perfume that smelled like mint and peaches. Her nearness
was having an effect on him. As Maggie never tired of point-
ing out, he hadn't been with a woman for quite a while.

"Now that I've met you," she purred, "I know that I made
the right choice. I read all about you, Jake. You're Native
American."

"Arapaho," he said.

"Is that like Navajo?" Her hand rested on her hip and she struck a calculated pose with her head cocked to one side. "I simply adore turquoise jewelry."

"Different tribe."

"Perhaps you could explain it to me. I'm very interested."

The woman was flirting her cute little tail off. Jake had three sisters; he knew how these feminine games were played. "Don't waste my time, Princess."

"Will you help me?"

"I'll do my job. My department and the local police and the FBI are looking for your brother, but a lot of time has passed. He might not even be in this area."

"He's not dead." She spoke with sudden sincerity. "If Amir had died, I would have felt his absence as surely as if part of my soul had been ripped away."

In the blink of an eye, she'd gone from flirty to serious. The transformation impressed him. "I'm sorry, Saida."

"Please. Tell me what happened. The truth."

He could give her that much. "It was late at night. The other royals and their entourages had returned to Wind River Ranch and Resort. Your brother set out in one of the limos with a driver. We don't know his destination. There was nothing remarkable about the area where the car bomb exploded."

Saida sucked in a breath. "And then?"

"The driver was killed in the explosion. There were indications that your brother was injured. His blood was found at the scene." He paused. "I can't show you the forensics reports, but the CSI was Jane Cameron, and she's good."

"What did she find?"

"Tire tracks showed an unidentified vehicle at the scene. A witness saw him exit the burning limo so we know he was still alive at that point, but there hasn't been any communication from him."

Her brow furrowed. "You're leaving out a lot."

"I am," he readily admitted. "I could write four books about the things that have happened since Amir disappeared."

"I have time," she said.

He glanced toward the house where his sister hovered in the doorway, waiting for him to bring their royal visitor inside. "It's best if you go to the resort where the other royals and their bodyguards are staying. You could be in danger."

"The attack on my brother might have been politically motivated," she said. "Our four nations…"

"COIN." He used the acronym. "The Coalition of Island Nations."

"Yes, COIN owns extensive oil resources. We have enemies, including the Russian mob, who would do anything to gain control of our wealth."

"And these dangerous people could come after you."

"Not me," she said. "As a woman, I have no power in Jamala. The leadership of the country would never pass to me. It's my destiny to be forever a princess. Never a true leader."

He heard an edge of bitterness in her voice. There was something fascinating about her, but he couldn't allow himself to get tangled in her web. "For tonight, you have a choice. Either you can go to the resort, or I can turn you over to the FBI for protective custody."

She waved her manicured hands in front of her face. Her fingernails had purple tips. "I can't be in custody. I have to be free to investigate."

"Then it's the resort." He walked toward the house. "Let me get my keys, and I'll follow you in my car to make sure you get there safely. Tomorrow, you can call me for an update."

"If you won't help, I'll pursue my own investigation."

That had to be one of the worst ideas he'd ever heard.

He couldn't imagine Saida flouncing through the streets of Dumont and asking questions. She'd stand out like a giraffe in a herd of prairie dogs.

Before he could object, she went to her car, started the engine and backed away from the porch.

He ran inside and grabbed his keys from the table by the door. Maggie glared at him. "What did you say to her? Why did you chase her off?"

"Because that woman is trouble."

"Lone wolf," she snapped. "You and Saida would make a really cute couple."

He couldn't believe she was playing matchmaker. "Trust me, Maggie. If I ever settle down, it won't be with a high-maintenance princess. No matter how pretty she is."

His sister beamed. "You think she's pretty?"

"She's not for me."

When he stepped outside onto the porch, he saw the taillights of a truck on the two-lane road beyond his driveway. A black sedan followed. Both were driving fast, and they seemed to be in formation—in pursuit of the princess.

Chapter Two

Angrier than she should have been, Saida glared through the windshield of the pitiful little rental car that had awaited her private jet at the Dumont airfield. She'd asked for an SUV, a vehicle with some muscle. But no! The Minister of Affairs in Jamala had made her travel arrangements, and Nasim thought big cars were un-princesslike. This silly little compact was his way of showing her who was the boss.

This time the joke was on Nasim. His insistence that she fly private rather than commercial allowed her to pack both of her handguns. If a firefight was necessary to rescue her brother, she wouldn't hesitate. All she needed was one person in her corner—a contact inside the investigation who could point her in the right direction. She had hoped that ally would be Jake Wolf, but she'd blown it with the sheriff.

When it came to personal negotiations, especially with men, she usually got what she wanted. She'd played the princess card and failed to impress him. Then she'd attempted to flirt. Catastrophe! Why, oh, why, had she made that silly comment about the Navajo turquoise jewelry? Playing dumb wasn't going to cut it with Jake. She should have known better.

Her internet research led her to surmise that Jake Wolf was incorruptible and unlikely to be swayed by bribes from those who had attacked her brother. She expected him to be a serious, responsible man.

What surprised her was his stunning physical presence. The internet photos hadn't done him justice. His eyes held the depth and fire of black diamonds. His square jaw was perfectly balanced by a high forehead and strong cheekbones. And that body? When she saw him shirtless with his jeans slung low on his hips, he had taken her breath away. His lean torso, hard muscles and smooth bronzed skin had almost made her forget why she'd come to this desolate place.

She inhaled a breath and exhaled slowly through her nostrils. Anger was futile. Instead, she needed to be calm and controlled. She needed a plan.

Though she'd programmed the location of the very exclusive, very posh Wind River Ranch and Resort into the GPS navigator in her rental car, she still wasn't sure if she should go there. The COIN royals wouldn't be happy to see her. Sheik Efraim Aziz, her brother's best friend, had been adamant about keeping her away. *Too bad, Efraim.*

It was time they all realized that she wasn't a child anymore. True, she'd made her share of mistakes. Her reputation as a socialite who paraded down red carpets and danced until dawn at trendy L.A. clubs was somewhat deserved. But she had also graduated from UCLA, and she'd earned top grades in her first year of law school. If given a chance, she'd prove that she could contribute to the welfare of COIN.

And she could help in the search for her brother.

The car's GPS navigational system said, "In two-point-four miles, turn left."

In her rearview mirror, she noticed headlights approaching. Though it was difficult to make out any details on this unlit road, the vehicle behind her appeared to be a truck and it was coming too fast. Inappropriate driving; this asphalt road wasn't the Swiss autobahn. Instinctively, she pressed down on the accelerator, hoping to make it to her turn before the truck caught up and caused her to crash.

Was this a drunk driver? Or a teenager out for a joyride? Saida was aware of the darker possibility. As a princess, she lived with the constant threat of being kidnapped for a royal ransom and had been trained in marksmanship, hand-to-hand combat and evasive driving techniques.

The headlights were on her tail. She was going fifty-eight miles per hour—an unsafe speed for making a ninety-degree turn on a narrow road.

"Turn left in one hundred feet," the GPS said.

Saida saw the stop sign and the intersection. She tapped the brake, hoping the truck behind her would slow down. No such luck. Its front bumper kissed the back of her car hard enough to give her a jolt. The driver wasn't following her by coincidence. He was pursuing her.

"Turn left now," said the GPS.

She cranked the steering wheel and swerved. Her light-weight rental car fishtailed wildly. Centrifugal force threatened to flip her car into a death roll. She maintained balance, controlled the turn and leveled out on a straightaway.

"In one-point-three miles, turn right."

The truck was still behind her. Even worse, another set of headlights appeared in the lane beside it and quickly pulled forward. If the second car got ahead of her, she'd be trapped between them.

She tromped on the accelerator. Seventy miles per hour. Seventy-five. Eighty. Going over a ridge, her vehicle was airborne. The car landed with a crash that stressed the shock absorbers.

"Turn right," the GPS said.

But she couldn't. It would be suicide to take the turn at this speed. The second vehicle—a dark sedan—remained in the lane for oncoming traffic. He pulled even with her rear fender.

The GPS system scolded, "You missed the turn."

"Shut up!"

Her training told her to hit the gas and zip into the other lane to block the second car, but she didn't have the horsepower to pull ahead. Panic flashed inside her head. *Think, Saida.*

In the backseat were two of the six suitcases she'd packed for this trip. Even if she could dig into the suitcase and reach her handguns, it wouldn't do much good. Her weapons weren't loaded.

The sedan passed her. Once it was in front of her, the driver slowed his speed. She was hemmed in with no room to maneuver, nowhere else to go. Beyond the shoulder of this road was a strip of land and a barbed-wire fence.

The truck pulled into the lane beside her. She lifted her foot from the accelerator and slowed. The truck matched her speed.

Before she felt the impact, she heard the grinding of metal against metal. He was forcing her off the road. Her tires crashed raggedly on the gravel shoulder.

Her foot jammed down hard on the brake.

The truck shot past her.

Her brake rotors screeched. She went into a skid.

The air bag exploded, blinding her and forcing her hands off the steering wheel. Her tires bounced off the road and over a ditch, throwing her car off balance. Before she tipped over, the car came to a full stop.

It was a miracle that she hadn't flipped over, that she didn't seem to be injured. Frantically, she batted at the air bag. Her fingers struggled to unfasten the seat belt. She had to run, had to get out of this car before her pursuers grabbed her.

The wail of a police siren cut through the air.

The bag deflated enough that she could see through the window. The taillights of the truck were zooming away from her. The other car had disappeared. They'd given up.

Adrenaline surged through her veins. She could have been killed, could have been kidnapped. Why was this happening? The inside of her head whirled in a dizzying tornado, and she gripped the wheel to stabilize herself.

The siren came closer, and she saw the flashing red and blue lights of a police vehicle.

Jake appeared outside her car window. He yanked on her door handle until it opened. "Saida, are you all right?"

Unable to speak, she could only nod.

When he touched her shoulder, she flinched. Every muscle in her body screamed with tension.

"You're going to be okay," he said. "Let go of the wheel."

She pried her fingers loose. Darkness pressed against her peripheral vision. She shook herself, fighting for control. *I won't pass out.* The idea of fainting into Jake's strong arms held a certain appeal, but she didn't want to show weakness. She wanted him to think of her as an equal.

Clearly, she said, "You got here just in time."

"Let's get you out of here." He took her hand to help her from the car. "We need to hurry. In case they come back."

That possibility was enough to get her moving. She lurched from her car and stood on shaky legs.

The lights from his vehicle showed the damage to her rental car. The trunk and rear bumper were caved in. A scrape gashed into the back door. It was sobering to see how close she'd come to disaster, but she couldn't allow herself to sink into helpless terror.

"Wait." She balked. "My luggage."

"I'll have someone come back for it."

"At least, I need my purse." She leaned into her wrecked car and reached across the driver's seat to grab her purse.

Her gaze slid toward the matched burgundy leather suitcases behind the front seat; she wanted her guns. "Can I get my luggage?"

"Forget it."

"We can leave the other bags in the trunk." With the rear end crushed in, it would take the Jaws of Life to retrieve those suitcases. "But I need that one."

"Why?"

It probably wouldn't be wise to tell him that she'd brought a couple of Berettas. Facing him, she drew up her shoulders and said, "I've got to have my makeup."

Without another word, he scooped her off her feet and threw her over his shoulder, carrying her like a sack of potatoes.

Upside down, she was shocked by his manhandling. Saida was a princess, after all. His arm pinned her legs so she couldn't kick. Her arms flailed wildly. With her purse, she whacked his butt. "Put me down."

"This is for your own good."

She'd heard those words before—many, many times before, and the statement never failed to infuriate her. *For my own good? Really?*

At his SUV, Jake dropped her to the ground, opened the passenger-side door and shoved her inside. While he circled around to the driver's side, she debated whether she should fling open the door, run to her car and grab her guns. Why had she thought Jake would be different? He was just like every other man in her life who wanted her to be a good girl and do as she was told.

The fear that threatened to swamp her consciousness was replaced by anger. It wasn't her fault that she'd been attacked. Given the circumstances, she'd handled herself well.

Jake slid behind the steering wheel. "Seat belt," he said.

Though outraged, she snapped the belt. "Apologize."

For an instant, his gaze locked with hers. "I won't say I'm sorry for saving your life."

He swung the SUV in a U-turn. Instead of using the police dispatch radio on the console, he took out his hands-free cell phone and made a call.

"Where are we going?" she demanded. "What are you doing?"

Ignoring her questions, he continued with his call. It seemed that he was giving someone directions to find her car.

"My luggage," she said. "Have them bring my luggage."

Jake lobbed a hostile glance in her direction and said to the person on the phone. "There are a couple of suitcases in the back. Bring them."

"There are other bags in the trunk," she said.

"How many?"

"Two in the back, four in the trunk, that's six altogether."

He raised an eyebrow. "Exactly how long were you planning to stay in Wyoming?"

"There's a certain standard of dress required of someone in my position. I can't throw on a pair of sweatpants and go waltzing out the door. I don't expect you to understand. Most men don't."

As he returned to his phone call, she sank back against the seat. If she told Jake that the reason she wanted her luggage wasn't just vanity, would it make a difference? Would he take her more seriously if he knew she'd come to Wyoming armed? Or would he insist on pushing her around? *For her own good.*

Jake ended his phone call and turned toward her. "I have to ask you some questions about what happened."

His tone was brisk and businesslike. The balance of power between them was all wrong. He was completely in charge, and that needed to change.

She grasped for control. "Tell me where we're going?"

"For now, we're headed back to my place."

Though her initial intention had been to link up with him, his choice of destination seemed odd. She'd been the victim of vehicular assault; a crime had been committed. "Shouldn't we be going to the police station?"

Instead of answering, he asked, "Can you describe the vehicles?"

"One was a truck. Not one of those huge heavy-duty monster trucks with big wheels. Just a pickup. It seemed kind of old, and I think it was black or dark gray."

"What made you think it was an older model?"

"It wasn't shiny. It looked used." She wished she'd been more observant. "I didn't get a license plate. And I'm not good at identifying make and model."

"What about the other vehicle?"

"A black sedan. A four-door." She shook her head. If it had been a Lamborghini or a Bugatti, she could have told him more. Most other cars looked the same. "It was similar to my rental car. Maybe it had tinted windows."

"It did," he said. "I only caught a glimpse of the truck when it came past my house, but I saw the sedan pretty clearly. They were driving in formation. It appeared to be an organized assault."

"They were working together. The sedan pulled in front. The truck tried to force me off the road."

The explanation sounded so bland—nothing at all like the harrowing reality of the chase. She called upon the regal poise that had been drummed into her since childhood to stay in control.

He asked, "Who knew you were coming to Wyoming?"

Though she hadn't informed anyone in the royal entourage, she hadn't made a secret of her plans. "The Minister of Affairs made my travel arrangements and reservations. I'm not sure if he talked to anyone else."

"Do you trust him?"

"Totally." She'd known Nasim all her life. "He'd never betray me."

"Someone did," he said. "Those cars were waiting for you. They knew you were coming."

They were approaching Jake's house. Again, she wondered, why had he brought her here instead of the police station? As part of a class in law enforcement, she'd been on a ride along; she knew he wasn't following standard police protocol. "You haven't turned on the police siren or the lights."

"That's right."

She pointed to the console on his dashboard. "When you contacted the person who would go to my car, you used your hands-free phone instead of calling your dispatcher."

"Right again."

She remembered what she'd read about him on the internet. Much of his campaign for sheriff had been based on a promise to clean up the corruption that had infected law enforcement in Wind River County. "Why are you avoiding the regular channels?"

"Here's what I think. The person who came after you in that truck is a local." He pulled up to the edge of the basketball court to park. "Until I find him, I'm only going to work with people I can count on. While you're here, I'd advise you to do the same."

She got the message.

There was no one she could trust.

And someone wanted to kill her.

Chapter Three

Whether he liked it or not, Jake was stuck with the princess. He couldn't hand her over to any other law enforcement agencies, not while he suspected corruption. Nor did he trust the hotel security at the Wind River Ranch and Resort. And the bodyguards for the royal entourage had the stink of traitor about them.

He escorted Saida to the safest room in his house—the guest bedroom on the second floor. Unlike his and Maggie's bedrooms, there was only one small window.

Keeping her here at his house wasn't a long-term solution. Not only did he have too many responsibilities as sheriff to act as her full-time bodyguard, but his home wasn't a fortress. Yeah, he had a security system that sounded an alarm if somebody tried to break in. But there was no defense against long-range rifles and snipers. Had the men who chased Saida wanted to kill her or to kidnap her? He suspected the latter. If their intent was murder, there were more effective methods than vehicular homicide.

He pulled the blinds and crossed the room to stand in the doorway. "You'll stay here until I know what's going on."

His humble guest bedroom with the scuffed knotty pine furniture probably wasn't the sort of accommodation she was accustomed to, but she didn't turn up her nose. She perched on the edge of the double bed and gave him a cooperative smile. "Is there anything I can do to help?"

"I have more questions."

"Perhaps I could have a glass of water." She slipped off her metallic jacket. Underneath, she wore a V-neck shirt of thin fabric that clung to her curves and was almost the same color as her skin—a naked shirt that sent his imagination into overdrive.

Regretfully, he tore his gaze away from the princess and looked over his shoulder at his sister who stood in the hallway. "Maggie, I'd like for you to go down to the kitchen and get something for Saida to drink and eat."

"My linguini?"

After Saida's nonsense about fussing with the makeup from her suitcase, he was tempted to torture her with Maggie's idea of gourmet. But that was too cruel. "Just a sandwich. Bring it up here."

She gave a quick nod and darted down the staircase.

He turned back to the princess. "I'll be honest with you, Saida. The best thing you could do is return to California."

"I'm not afraid." A blush warmed her cheeks, but her golden eyes were calm. "I won't leave until I find my brother."

He'd expected as much and wouldn't waste another breath trying to convince her. "Do you have any idea why those men came after you?"

"Not a clue."

"Since we don't know the why, we'll concentrate on how. How did those guys know you were in town?"

"Flying into the airport in a private jet might not have been the most subtle way for me to arrive." She pulled up her leg and unfastened the strap on one of her platform sandals. Her foot was delicate with a high arch, and she wore a thin silver chain around her ankle. "The jet wasn't my idea. Nasim insisted."

"The Minister of Affairs in Jamala," he said. "Would he have told anyone about your arrival?"

"He might have informed Efraim." She shrugged. "Don't waste time suspecting Nasim. His primary concern in life is my welfare."

Jake wasn't so sure. "Tell me about him."

"When I was younger, Nasim was a combination body-guard and mother hen. He accompanied me everywhere, even to Beverly Hills—a place he utterly despised. The only thing he enjoyed about Southern California was the freeway system, which he considered a challenge. He always drove as though on a military campaign and bragged whenever he shaved a few minutes off the drive time."

When Jake had gone after her, he'd been on a rise overlooking the road and had been able to see last part of the chase. She'd maneuvered her car like a Demolition Derby expert; her decision to hit the brakes had probably saved her from a rollover. "Did Nasim teach you to drive?"

"He trained me in evasive driving techniques, and in other skills to protect myself from kidnapping. Do you think that's what was intended? Kidnapping?"

In spite of his earlier conclusion, he didn't answer her question. They weren't working together. "Do you have reservations at the resort?"

"Yes." She removed her other shoe and massaged her toes. "Maybe someone at the hotel leaked my name to the enemies of COIN."

"It's possible." Over the past few days, his men had done a thorough job of vetting the employees at the resort. He doubted that any of them were working with the bad guys, but somebody could have mentioned her arrival. Or the reservation desk computer could have been hacked.

She frowned. "I should have told Nasim to use a fake name."

"Do you often use an alias?"

"Of course," she said as though assumed names were a normal part of life. "I travel incognito to throw the paparazzi off my trail."

"Too late for that. They're already here." The reporters and photographers who had showed up in Dumont at the first sign of trouble were as pesky as a swarm of gnats.

"There's one paparazzo who is particularly annoying. His name is Danny Harold." Her upper lip curled in disgust. "He specializes in photographs of royalty, and he'll do anything to get an exclusive shot."

Maggie came back into the room carrying a tray. "You always look gorgeous in the tabloids. I remember a photo of you standing on tiptoe to kiss one of the Lakers."

"Don't remind me. That picture started a million rumors about royal weddings, even though I only dated the guy twice."

"The Lakers?" In spite of himself, Jake was starstruck. "You've gone out with players on the winningest franchise in professional basketball?"

"If you come to L.A., I can get you courtside seats."

"Damn." There were advantages to knowing a princess.

Maggie placed the tray on the bed and shoved a paper plate toward him. "Eat."

Absently, he took a bite from the sandwich. When this investigation was over, he fully intended to take the princess up on her offer. It was almost worth all the strife these royals had caused to get courtside seats.

Maggie handed a plate to Saida. "Tell me a couple of your aliases."

"As a child, I used to watch a lot of American movies. That's when I first fell in love with this country. So I use movie names. Dorothy Gale, Bridget Jones, Holly Golightly. And, of course, Elle Woods."

"Of course," Maggie said.

Jake had no idea what they were talking about. "Elle Woods?"

"The heroine of *Legally Blonde*," his sister informed him. "Everybody thought she was a ditzy blonde, but she went to Harvard Law School and outsmarted them all."

"A lighthearted film with a significant message." Saida slid an accusing glance in his direction. "It's easy to underestimate someone based on stereotypes. Sometimes, the dumb blonde is the smartest person in the room. And the pampered princess is the most resourceful."

Touché. He knew he'd been guilty of taking her lightly. There might be more depth to this princess than he'd thought.

Maggie said, "I love your pinkie ring. Is the design a royal crest?"

He'd noticed the ring before—a black onyx stone with a silver design that he'd at first thought was a butterfly. Looking closer, he saw that it was crossed swords.

Saida gestured gracefully, displaying the ring. "It's similar to the crossed scimitars that are part of Saudi Arabia's coat of arms, but this ring has no special meaning. I just liked the design, and I have earrings to match."

"Does Jamala have crown jewels?" Maggie asked.

"An extensive collection, most of which is in the National Museum. There's a story behind the Farrah Blue diamond. Any woman who wears the gem is guaranteed to have masculine children." She gave Maggie a grin. "As if that's good."

"Tell me more," Maggie said.

Jake finished his sandwich. Though she'd subtly rebuked him for stereotyping, he couldn't help comparing Saida to the princess in *One Thousand and One Arabian Nights*. If he didn't get away from her soon, he'd stay all night, lulled into a trance by her cultured voice. "Excuse me, ladies. I have work to do."

Downstairs, he went through the house—pulling the curtains, locking the windows and dragging his thoughts back to the situation at hand. He couldn't allow himself to be captivated by Saida's charms or her promise of courtside seats. The fact that this kidnap attempt had been made here instead of California indicated that this crime was tied to all the others, including her brother's disappearance. He needed solutions.

The antidote to Saida came when he heard his deputy pull into the driveway outside his house. Kent Wheeler was Jake's most trusted employee and the person he'd called on his phone right after leaving the scene of the crash.

He opened the front door for the stocky blue-eyed deputy who usually wore a cowboy hat to cover his bald spot. Though out of uniform, Wheeler's appearance was crisp and neat. His wife always ironed his jeans to leave a crease.

"What's up, Sheriff?"

Before Jake could answer, Saida was halfway down the stairs.

"Good evening, sir." She bestowed a mesmerizing smile on Wheeler. "Have you brought my luggage?"

"Yes, ma'am." Wheeler wasn't the sort of guy who would ever cheat on his wife, but he was staring at the princess with unabashed appreciation.

"Later," Jake growled. "We'll bring your suitcases upstairs later."

"I appreciate it so much." She turned and trotted back to the guest bedroom.

Staring after her, Wheeler said, "She's something else."

"She's a load of trouble," Jake said. "That's Princess Saida Khalid, the sister of Amir. She was driving that car when it was forced off the road."

"A real live princess. Whoa, I never thought I'd meet somebody like her."

Wheeler remained at the foot of the staircase, looking up in case she might reappear. Jake might have to use his stun gun to bring his deputy back to earth. "Did you contact Jane Cameron?"

"Yes, sir. The forensic team arrived at the scene of the crash just as I was taking the luggage from the backseat. Jane wasn't happy about having me disturb her evidence."

She was involved with Prince Stefan Lutece of Kyros. Ever since they hooked up, the formerly plain Jane had been beaming and dropping hints that she'd be leaving her job and moving to one of the COIN nations. Though he didn't doubt Jane's professionalism, she'd probably been in the arms of her prince when she got the call. Jake couldn't keep Saida's arrival a secret; he needed to inform the COIN royals as soon as possible. Sheik Efraim seemed to be closest to Saida and her brother.

He sank into a chair beside the fireplace and checked the clock on the mantel. It was after eleven. This wouldn't be a pleasant call. He and Efraim had argued before. They'd buried the hatchet, but not too deeply.

Using his cell phone, he contacted the front desk at the resort and left a message for Efraim to call him. "Tell him it's an emergency."

Disconnecting the call, he looked toward his deputy. "I'm putting you in charge of this investigation, Wheeler. Hand-pick the team you work with. We need to be careful about who we trust."

"Understood. We don't want a repeat of what happened with Amos Andrews."

Andrews, a Dumont policeman, had played a part in the first wave of attacks and had threatened Jane Cameron's life. In jail, he'd committed suicide under suspicious circumstances. Jake wondered if he'd been murdered to insure his silence—murdered by someone on the inside, another traitor.

Though he'd been sheriff for nearly a year, Jake still felt the simmering resentment from those on his staff who were loyal to the former sheriff. Every day was a battle to earn their respect. Not only was he the new guy but he was Arapaho, and old prejudices sometimes flared back to life.

Wheeler took a small spiral notebook from his shirt pocket. "Where should I start?"

"We're looking for a black or gray truck with damage on the passenger side. And a black, four-door sedan." The car had whipped past his house so fast that Jake hadn't recognized the make or model. "Tomorrow morning, you can check with the local car rental places for information on midsize sedans."

"Got it." Wheeler scribbled in his notebook.

"Somebody knew about the princess's arrival, which means there's a leak. You'll need to talk to the reservations people at the resort."

"Again?"

"You never know. They're supposed to be discreet, but somebody might have gotten all excited and blabbed. I guess she's some kind of celebrity. She dated a guy on the Lakers."

"The Lakers?" His eyes popped wide open. "Whoa."

Jake wondered if his own reaction had been that obvious. "You look like you might run home and tell your wife."

"No, sir, not my wife. Not unless I wanted to get whacked over the head with a frying pan. But I might be tempted to tell some of the guys."

That was probably how the information had gotten out, but they needed to make sure there wasn't a more nefarious explanation. "I'll talk to the FBI. They can use their fancy tracing equipment to see if the reservations computer at the resort was hacked."

From upstairs, he heard his sister giggle. At least somebody was having fun.

Jake's phone rang, and he answered. "Jake Wolf."

"This is Efraim Aziz. What is the big emergency?"

"Princess Saida is in town. She's at my house."

There was a moment of silence.

Efraim said, "My advice to you, Sheriff, is to saddle up and ride as fast and as far as you can."

Chapter Four

Sitting cross-legged on the double bed in the guest room, Saida was enjoying her conversation with Jake's sister. Their topics ranged from fashion and shoes to cultural norms in Jamala and the rights of women. If this had been a purely social occasion, Saida might have relaxed, but she was edgy—distracted by what was going on downstairs. With the door to the bedroom open, she could hear the murmur of male voices as Jake conferred with his deputy.

As usual, she was being excluded, and there seemed to be nothing she could do about it. Until Jake said it was safe, he wouldn't allow her to leave the guest bedroom. He'd already shown himself to be capable of throwing her over his shoulder. What would come next? Tying her to a chair?

She stretched out her legs. "I want your brother to invite me into his investigation, to work with him and find Amir. How should I approach him?"

"With a baseball bat to knock some sense into his stubborn head. Forget about Jake. Tell me how you ended up in Beverly Hills."

"While I was in boarding school in Switzerland, I made friends with a girl from Los Angeles. Since I was already in love with American movies, California seemed like a natural destination for me. I begged until I was allowed to go to a private high school in Los Angeles." She smiled at Maggie.

"Now it's your turn. You grew up on the reservation. What was it like?"

"So boring. Actually, I'm kind of like you. By the time I was in high school, my older sister was working in Denver. That's where I went to high school."

"In a way, we're both expatriates."

"In a way." Maggie nodded. "Why did you come to our house as soon as you got into town?"

"I looked Jake up on the internet. He seemed like someone I could trust. When he was running for sheriff, there was an interesting endorsement from someone named Oscar."

"Poor little Oscar."

In his endorsement, he hadn't sounded poor at all. The accompanying photograph was very Armani. "He's an attorney in Cheyenne, right?"

"When Jake met him, Oscar Pollack wasn't what you'd call a success story. He was a skinny little runt, too nervous to take his eyes off his own toes. He and Jake were both in their first year of college at UDub and—"

"Wait." Saida held up her hand. "UDub?"

"University of Wyoming in Laramie," Maggie said. "That's where I'm going, too. Anyway, Jake was on a basketball scholarship and joined the coolest frat on campus. After the first game of the season, everybody knew him. Jake Wolf—the Wolfman—was a star. Oscar was an insignificant speck."

The college hierarchy was much the same everywhere. Though Saida had never lived on the UCLA campus or bothered with sororities, she was one of the in-crowd. "What happened?"

"One night, Jake went to a bar with his buddies, even though he doesn't drink. Oscar was working there, bussing tables. He accidentally spilled beer on a big ape who took it personally. He and his pals followed Oscar after his shift was over. Oscar made it to his car, but that didn't stop the apes. They kicked dents into the car doors and threw rocks. They busted the windshield."

Saida guessed what came next. "Jake stepped in."

"Oh, yeah. To hear Oscar tell the story, you'd think my brother was some kind of superhero, taking on three big guys at once. According to Jake, they were stumbling around and drunk—but not so smashed that they didn't recognize the Wolfman. It turned out that one of the ape's pals was in Jake's frat."

Noble actions often came with a price. "Did they try to kick him out?"

"Jake quit before they could ask him to leave, and he was glad to do it. He didn't want to be part of a group that condoned bullies." Maggie beamed a smile. She was proud of her big brother, deservedly so. "It all turned out for the best."

"How so?"

"You can't tell Jake I said this, but he was never destined for the NBA. He moved to a different frat that was more focused on academics than sports. His good grades served him better than a nonexistent sports career."

"And Oscar went to law school," Saida concluded.

"He turned out great, has a wonderful family. And he's a big deal in state politics," Maggie said. "He thinks Jake can be the first Native American elected governor if he learns how to play politics."

Diplomacy was something Saida understood. "I could teach him a thing or two."

"He's going to need a boost," Maggie said. "With everything that's happened recently, Jake's reputation as a lawman is at an all-time low."

Saida regretted the trouble caused by the COIN royals. It was enough to stir up turmoil and strife in their own nations without spreading their problems to Wyoming. "When I find my brother, we'll make amends. I promise you, Maggie. Amir and I will make this right."

She heard someone coming up the stairs and hopped off the bed as Jake pushed the door open. His clenched jaw and the parallel frown lines between his eyebrows told her that he wasn't in the mood for a reasonable chat.

"You can both come downstairs," he said. "I have a deputy posted out front and another by the barn. Nobody but a damn fool would attack when they are so sure to be caught."

She picked up her sandals by the straps. "I'm sorry to have added to your problems."

"Forget it."

He gestured for them to leave the room. Maggie went first, and Saida followed. Her brain was in high gear, trying to figure out a way to convince Jake that she was worthy of participating in his investigation. If she could get him to listen, just for a moment…

She looked up at him. Trapped in the door frame, they were standing close together—much too close. She hadn't meant to seduce him, but there was a definite attraction between them. The heat radiating from his body sparked a flame inside her, and the fire spread in a whoosh, consuming the air in her lungs. With an effort, she pushed out a question. "Did you find out how those men knew I was coming to town?"

"The leak," he said.

"Yes."

"We're considering several possibilities."

So was she, but her considerations had nothing to do with investigating and everything to do with his lips, his chest, his scent. She'd been around handsome men before—actors, athletes and male models—but she'd never been so affected.

She took a step into the hallway, putting distance between

herself and the sheriff. "I have an idea. A way we can find the leak."

"I spoke to Sheik Efraim. He's coming to pick you up."

That bit of news hit her like a splash of ice water. As soon as Jake delivered her to Efraim, she'd be trapped in a velvet prison, surrounded by bodyguards. She needed to take action, to force Jake to listen.

In the middle of the living room, she spotted the two suitcases that had been in the backseat of her rental car. In a few minutes, she'd locate her weapons. If nothing else, she'd be armed. But first, she needed to get Jake's attention.

"There's something I need to discuss with you, Jake." She went to the door and opened it. "Can we talk on the porch? You said it was safe."

"I did say that." And he looked like he regretted it.

She stepped outside into the night. Her gaze swept through a stand of pine trees and bushes on the opposite side of the driveway. Her plan was almost certain to tick him off, but he wasn't leaving her another option. If she didn't do something, he'd ship her off with Efraim and never speak to her again.

Standing under the porch light, she tilted her chin so her features would be clearly illuminated. She'd been photographed hundreds of times and knew how to pose.

When he joined her, she set aside her natural attraction to him. Now was not the time for lust. Not real lust, anyway. With the skill of a choreographer, she positioned him.

"What's this about?" he asked.

"Finding the leak."

She reached up and stroked his cheek. Looking up at him, she leaned closer, closer, closer.

She heard a clicking noise coming from the trees and a flash. Then a second flash.

Jake reacted instantly. Shielding her with his body, he yanked her arm and shoved her through the open door into the house. He pivoted and crouched. In two steps, he crossed the porch and vaulted the railing.

Saida bit her lower lip to keep from grinning. Her plan had worked.

RUNNING HARD, JAKE CHARGED across the basketball court and rushed into the thicket of pine trees opposite his house. Low branches on the bushes snapped against his legs as he dodged through the tree trunks. Anger surged through him. They'd been ambushed. In spite of his precautions, someone had gotten close enough to shoot. The weapon had been a camera not a gun. But the intent was the same.

The moonlight was enough for him to see the back of his quarry. A man in a black windbreaker and a black knit cap, he moved though the trees with a clumsy halting gait. His arms thrashed at low hanging branches. This was a man unfamiliar with forests and uneven terrain.

Jake was gaining on him. These mountains were his home. Since childhood, he'd been running through these forests. He knew how to place his feet, when to dodge and when to leap.

The man in black broke out of the trees into the open. Directly ahead of him was the barbed-wire fence that separated Jake's property from his neighbor's. As he swerved to avoid crashing headlong into the fence, he stumbled and fell to his hands and knees.

Jake shouted a warning. "Stop. Police."

The man staggered upright. He was breathing hard. "Don't shoot."

"Show me your hands."

"I'm a photographer." He pointed to the camera hanging on a strap around his neck. In his left hand, he held some kind of flash device. "I'm not going to hurt anybody. I just wanted a picture of the princess."

Jake didn't have a set of handcuffs with him, but he didn't think he'd need them. His rage was enough to ensure this guy wouldn't resist. "Come with me."

"Fine. Whatever."

Jake tore the flash from his hand. "Give me the camera."

"I got a great photo of you and Saida. And I mean great." He sucked down a breath. "You look good together. You might not know this, but you're developing a fan base. The women in my office are watching your daily briefings and they want more pictures of the sexy sheriff of Wind River County."

Oh, swell. "Your camera. Now."

"Awright, awright." He took the camera from his neck and handed it over. "Be careful with the equipment. It's top-of-the-line, expensive."

Jake glared at this unshaven little ferret with the long, greasy, blond ponytail. "I've seen you hanging around at the resort."

"Danny Harold," he introduced himself. "Saida knows me. I've taken about a million photos of the princess."

And she must have known that the paparazzo would be lurking outside the house. When she lured Jake onto the porch and touched his cheek so sweetly, she'd been setting him up for a photo op. She'd conned him. His anger at her translated into a growl at the man in his custody. "Danny Harold, you're under arrest."

"For what?" he yelped.

"Consider yourself lucky, it wasn't so long ago that we shot trespassers."

Jake marched him through the trees and back to the house. The walk gave him time to cool down, and that was good. He was outraged. The way she'd manipulated him with this stunt went too far. The last thing he needed was some high-maintenance princess flouncing around and making ridiculous demands. What the hell had she been thinking? What did she hope to gain from Danny Harold?

Kent Wheeler stood on the porch, gun in hand. Though the brim of his hat shielded his eyes, his frustration was evident. "Sorry, Sheriff. I don't know how this creep got so close."

"Not your fault." Jake shoved Danny toward him. "Cuff him and put him in your car."

While Danny squawked about freedom of the press and how he didn't mean any harm, Jake mounted the steps to the porch and entered the house. Maggie and Saida were sitting at the dining room table with coffee mugs in front of them. The princess rose to her feet and adjusted the fur collar of the vest she'd put on over her naked shirt. Her posture was perfect, and her attitude was so imperial that she could have been wearing a crown.

He wanted to tear away that composure and get to the truth. He placed the camera equipment on the table and said to his sister, "Give us some privacy."

"Sure thing."

When Maggie stepped up beside him and touched his arm, he almost flinched. Holding his anger in check was taking all his willpower. Her touch morphed into a sisterly hug that felt like a straitjacket. He assured her, "I'm fine."

She looked up at him with worried eyes. "Can I get anything for you? Coffee? A sandwich? Linguini?"

"Get out of here, sis."

He waited until Maggie had disappeared up the stairs and he heard the door to her room close. Then he confronted Saida.

"I want an explanation, Princess."

"I'M HAPPY TO EXPLAIN." Saida remained standing at the table. "Danny Harold is the bane of my existence. He's after me all the time, stalking me with his camera. I suspected that he'd find a way to get close. If I gave him a photo opportunity that he couldn't resist, he'd reveal himself."

Finally, Jake had gotten a direct answer from her. Not that it made any sense. She hated Danny, but she wanted to see him. *What?* He homed in on the important fact. "You were trying to lure him into the open."

"Yes."

"And you used me to do it."

"You gave me no choice," she said. "You refused to listen to me. I have a plan."

A headache throbbed behind his eyes. All her fancy footwork was making him dizzy. "I'm listening now. What's this big plan of yours?"

"The time of my arrival was leaked to the men who chased me. If someone who works at the resort or the airport was responsible, that person must have passed their information to the paparazzi, as well."

"How do you figure?"

"People like Danny pay well for tips." With an elegant gesture, she tucked her shiny, black hair behind her ear. "If we ask him the right questions, he'll identify his source."

Either Jake was losing his mind or she was making sense. "Talking to Danny Harold is actually a decent plan."

"So I'm right."

"Don't push it." He went to the door and called to Deputy Wheeler. "Bring Danny in here."

"Can I interrogate him?" she asked. "This is my plan, after all."

"What do you know about interrogation?"

"I just finished my first year at UCLA law school. All A's except for a B in torts. I hate torts."

Law school? "Why are you studying law?"

"I hope to reform the legal system in my country and in the other COIN nations. I want to do something useful."

He stalked past her and went into the kitchen, hoping to put distance between them. He didn't want to be sucked into her life story.

"Right now, all that's expected of me is to appear on red carpets and attend charity and political events," she said as she trailed behind him.

"That doesn't sound so bad."

"It's a lot of work. I have to spend the whole day being coiffed, fitted and painted with makeup. Five-inch heels are gorgeous but painful. You should try it sometime."

He had no intention of walking a mile in her stilettos. "If you hate it so much, why do it?"

"It's my duty. I'm a de facto ambassador, making contacts for Jamala. It never hurts to remind people in America of our existence. Tourism is an important industry for my country."

He opened the cherry cabinet next to the sink, took down a striped ceramic mug and filled it to the brim with coffee. Not that he needed a wake-me-up. His adrenaline was still pumping from chasing Danny and from dealing with the princess. She was too clever, too manipulative and far too appealing.

"Will you allow me to speak to Danny?" she asked. "Can I at least stay in the room?"

Her cool, caramel eyes shone with confidence. After all that had happened, her poise remained unruffled. "We'll both question him."

"Oh, Jake. I'm so glad we'll be working together."

He had the sinking feeling that he'd somehow been recruited into a partnership he didn't want. And if he tried to explain that they weren't a team, she'd find a way to tighten the leash. How the hell had the princess gotten the upper hand?

Chapter Five

Before he became sheriff, Jake had spent seven years on the Cheyenne police force and had worked his way up to detective. Never once had he allowed the victim to participate in the interrogation of a witness. Nor had he ever conducted an investigation from his house.

Proper procedure was being shredded. But he wanted answers, and he had the feeling that Danny Harold would respond to the princess.

Deputy Wheeler escorted Danny, still in handcuffs, through the front door and sat him at the far end of the dining room table. The grungy little ferret beamed a toothy grin as soon as he spotted Saida. "There she is. Princess Saida Khalid of Jamala. You've always been one of my favorites."

"I can't say the same about you."

"Come on, Princess. You like the attention, even if you won't cop to it. Why else do you wear the short skirts and those sexy necklines? You're one hell of a hot little number."

"Show some respect." Jake snatched the black knit cap from Danny's head. "Otherwise, you'll be spending the rest of the week in jail."

"You don't scare me. I have every right to do what I do. It's called freedom of the press."

Jake doubted that the Founding Fathers had paparazzi in mind when they drafted the First Amendment. "This isn't about your photography. You trespassed on my property. And you broke branches on my bushes. That's vandalism. If I charge you, it's two weeks in the county jail."

"That's not fair," he whined. "You can't—"

Jake slammed the cap down on the table. "I'm the law in this county. You'd be wise to cooperate."

Danny pulled back his chin like a turtle retreating into his shell. "What do you want from me?"

"First, you tell Princess Saida that you're sorry."

He glared at her. "Yeah, right. Sorry."

As apologies went, that was pathetic. But Jake didn't press for more. He nodded to Wheeler. "Take off the cuffs."

As soon as Danny's hands were free, he made a grab for his camera that was still resting on the table.

Jake snatched it away. "You don't get this until you answer some questions."

"Whatever. Let's get this over with."

Jake looked toward the princess. "Go ahead."

"Thank you, Sheriff Wolf." Apparently, Saida thought that using his title gave more gravity to her interrogation. "Let's start at the beginning, Danny. When did you arrive in Wind River County?"

"As soon as I knew the princes were coming here." Proudly, he said, "I have good contacts in Europe, and they told me about the COIN summit. I was one of the first on the scene. The publicity from the explosions and shootings were a bonus."

"And you've been taking pictures ever since you arrived."

"You know I have. That's my bread and butter."

"Huh," Deputy Wheeler said. "Can you really make a living doing this?"

"I get decent bucks for pictures of royalty, especially in Europe. The COIN princes have a lot going for them—they're handsome, titled and single."

It dawned on Jake that Danny's photos might come in handy. He might have caught something that would help the investigation. He went to the side table and picked up his sister's laptop. "Show us some of these moneymaking photos."

"With pleasure." Danny rubbed his hands together, talking while he plugged his digital photo card into the laptop. "Right now, I'm on assignment from a British tabloid. They're picking up my expenses. Whatever they don't use, I'm free to sell elsewhere. Here we go. That's from a couple of days ago."

The first photo showed only two people. One of them was a woman who worked at the resort. With her was one of the twin Cavanaugh princes, probably Antoine. They appeared to be holding hands and didn't seem aware of the camera.

Saida cooed. "That's so sweet."

Jake ignored the fact that Danny probably hadn't gotten a release for this picture. It wasn't his problem unless somebody pressed charges. "Let's see a group shot."

"Why?"

"You claim to be the best. Let's see what you can do when there's competition."

Danny scrolled through several other pictures until he found one of both Cavanaugh princes standing with other people around. Jake recognized a couple of faces in the crowd. Burt Maddox, the former sheriff, was talking to one of the guys who worked for him. Chad Granger, a troublemaker who'd been in and out of jail, slouched at the edge of the crowd. Sheik Efraim was walking away. There were other faces he'd like to identify.

"That's enough." Danny removed the photo card. "If you want to see more, you need a subpoena."

The little weasel knew his rights. Jake didn't need to get embroiled in a lawsuit with a British tabloid. But he was short on suspects; Danny's photos could help. "I'd appreciate your consent."

"I'll make a deal," Danny said. "Let me use that photo of you and Saida on the porch. That shot is a moneymaker, worthy of front page in the tabloids. And on the entertainment TV programs."

"It's all right with me," Saida said. "I can deal with it."

"I can't." The most difficult part of Jake's campaign for sheriff had been the publicity. Some of his Arapaho ancestors believed that when someone took your picture they captured a piece of your soul. "Print that photo, and I'll sue."

Danny backed off. "No need to get all self-righteous and litigious."

Jake wished he didn't have to care about public opinion. He wanted to be his own man. But he was sheriff, and that meant he had to hold to a certain standard of behavior. Not that the photo of him and Saida was porn, but he couldn't afford to be front-page news in a tabloid.

The princess spoke up, "Danny, I have a question for you."

"Shoot."

Though her voice stayed calm, she betrayed her nervousness by twisting the black onyx ring on her pinkie. "How did you find out that I was coming to Wyoming?"

"I've got my sources," Danny admitted. "And I'm staying close to the resort so I'm on top of things. It wasn't hard to find out that you'd made a reservation. You're a celebrity. Three or four of the staff mentioned your arrival."

Jake believed him. The Wind River Ranch and Resort was a high-class place, but Dumont was a small town where gossip spread faster than wildfire. If the women on the staff were anything like his sister, they'd be excited about the princess. Unfortunately, Danny's information wasn't much help in pinpointing the men who came after Saida.

"You heard I had a reservation," she said. "Then what did you do?"

"I was at the private airfield when your plane landed. I

thought I might get some pictures, but you hustled into the rental car too fast."

"At the airfield," she said, "did you notice anyone else watching my plane arrive?"

He folded his arms across his skinny chest and leaned back in the chair. "Maybe I did."

Now they were getting somewhere. Jake was tempted to step in and take over the interrogation, but Saida seemed to be asking the right questions.

"Tell me about these others who were watching," she said. "What did they look like? What kind of vehicles were they driving?"

Danny smirked. "This is important, huh?"

She sat in the chair beside him. Though she didn't actually touch him, she reached out with the full force of her personal charisma. "I must know what you saw and who you saw."

Danny's expression changed. Gazing at her, he seemed to be melting. An involuntary smile tugged at the corner of his mouth. His smug attitude disappeared as he leaned forward, wanting to be close to her.

And the princess reeled him in. Her left hand rested on the table, just beyond his grasp. With the other hand, she raked her shimmering black hair away from her cheek as she tilted her head to one side. She lowered her eyelids and slowly looked up at him.

A worshipful sigh pushed through his lips. "Oh, Saida."

"Please tell me, Danny."

"It's a private airfield," he said, "so there isn't a lot of security. I parked in the lot and walked closer. I stayed in the shadows, out of sight. After you got into your rental car, I talked to one of the guys who unloaded your luggage. He told me you were going to see Sheriff Wolf."

"Did you see him speak to anyone else?"

Danny shook his head. "I figured you were going to meet

the sheriff at his office, and I wasted a lot of time driving into Dumont before I came here."

"Other than the men who worked at the airfield, did you see anyone?"

"No, and I'm aware of other people. I try to be first on the scene with the exclusive photos."

Jake glanced toward his deputy and gave a nod. They needed to add another item to their list of things to do: talk to the workers at the airfield and find out who else they'd talked to.

"There's one more thing," Danny said. "When I went to the parking lot, I almost got run down. This guy was hauling ass. He was in a black truck."

That pretty much cinched it. Jake knew how the bad guys got their information. The real question was: Why? Why were they after the princess?

SAIDA WISHED SHE HAD gotten more from her interrogation of Danny. He had been in Wyoming from the start, snapping photos, and she wanted to look through those pictures and search for clues. She'd taken Danny's card with the intention of arranging a meeting with him later at the resort.

Before Deputy Wheeler had escorted Danny from the house, Jake had insisted that he delete the photographs he'd taken of them on the porch. She was glad. The last time she'd been the starring topic of entertainment news, it had taken a toll on her privacy. A suggested romance with the handsome sheriff would distract from the important matter of finding her brother.

With Wheeler and Danny gone and Maggie still upstairs in her bedroom, Saida found herself alone in the living room with Jake. She had to take advantage of this moment before Sheik Efraim arrived. Somehow, she had to solidify her relationship with the sheriff and convince him that she was indispensable to the investigation.

"That went well," she said. "Now we know how the bad guys found out about my arrival. I'm good at interrogating, aren't I?"

He went to a chair by the fireplace and sat. "I'm guessing that you're a woman who knows how to get what she wants."

"A useful ability in an investigation."

"I suppose."

He had put up a shield to deflect anything and everything she said. Jake wouldn't be won over by flattery. Nor would he be impressed if she batted her eyelashes and bestowed a thousand sweet smiles. Her last resort was logic.

She sat on the end of the sofa closest to his chair. "I've been asking myself why my brother came here. He's a sensible man and never does anything on a whim. Why did he choose this place for the summit meeting?"

"The Wind River Ranch and Resort has a fine reputation." Jake eyed her with suspicion. "No one seems to know exactly why he chose the place."

"As his sister, I have a deeper understanding of Amir than anyone else."

"When was the last time you saw him?"

"It was eight or nine months ago. He was in the United States on business and spent a few days with me in Beverly Hills." That time was a bit of a blur. "I was so busy starting law school that I wasn't very attentive."

If she had been more alert, she might have picked up clues. It pained her to think that she might have missed something that could save her brother's life.

Jake asked, "What did you talk about?"

They'd argued about her tabloid notoriety. Amir thought it was high time for her to settle down. When she'd said the same to him, he had seemed secretive. "I had a feeling about him. There was something different. Maybe he was involved with a woman."

"I don't know your brother," Jake said, "but I've seen how women react to the other COIN princes. I'm guessing that Amir had plenty of girlfriends."

"He has a reputation. Some refer to him as a black sheep. But it's not true. My brother is nothing like our father. He was the great womanizer."

Her father had disappointed her in so many ways. She tried not to think about him, opening that door released a gush of regret. "My father had a great fondness for the American West. He often told us stories about cowboys and ranches."

"Maybe he spent time in the West," Jake suggested.

"As a young man, he came to the Rocky Mountains." One of the few occasions when her father paid attention to her was when she was learning to ride. "He told me about cowgirls. How they could ride and use a rope as well as any man."

"And shoot," Jake said. "Like Annie Oakley."

"Oh, yes. I watched the movie." She'd loved the stories and the independent spirit of Western women. "I wanted to be like those cowgirls. Amir is nine years older than I am, but he would play cowboy with me."

"Did your father visit Wyoming?"

"I'm not sure," she said. "I was very young when he told me those stories."

"We can ask around," Jake said. "Some of the old-timers might remember."

"A wonderful idea."

She noticed that he'd said "we." He was including her in the investigation, and that was a step in the right direction. Everything was going her way. She'd work with Jake—a prospect that pleased her on several levels. They'd find Amir, and he'd be all right. There would be happy endings all around.

The front door swung open. Sheik Efraim Aziz of Nadar strode into the living room.

She braced herself for the impending storm.

Chapter Six

Efraim was different. Saida saw a huge change in the tall, dark, handsome sheik she'd known all her life. For one thing, he was dressed like a cowboy in jeans, a Western-cut shirt and casual jacket. Unbelievable! Efraim despised and distrusted everything American and had given her no end of grief about her decision to live in California. And here he was, looking like he'd sauntered in from a rodeo.

His posture was still ramrod-straight and his black eyes burned with intensity, but his granite jaw was relaxed. He was somehow...gentler.

She also observed a degree of animosity between Jake and Efraim as they exchanged tight-lipped nods. Instead of crossing the living room to shake hands, Jake stayed in his position beside the fireplace, and Efraim made no attempt to approach the sheriff.

Instead, he came toward her. "Saida, when will you learn to listen to me? You should have stayed in Beverly Hills."

"It's nice to see you, too."

"You shouldn't be here," he said coldly.

"I'm not going."

"We'll see about that." With a smooth gesture, he presented the petite blonde woman who accompanied him. She was also wearing jeans but she had on a tailored, professional-looking black blazer. "I'd like to introduce Callie McGuire, an assistant to the Secretary of Foreign Affairs."

As he spoke her name, Efraim's voice warmed. Someone who didn't know him as well as Saida wouldn't have noticed the difference in his tone, but she'd grown up around Efraim. When she was a little girl, he and her brother were teenagers. She had followed the two young men everywhere. They paid no attention to Amir's tagalong little sister, but she watched them carefully, memorizing their moods and their language. She'd copied their swagger when she walked. And she'd been reprimanded for using curse words she heard from them.

Efraim had crooned Callie McGuire's name. Combined with his newfound gentleness and the cowboy clothes, there was only one logical conclusion: Sheik Efraim had fallen in love with an American woman.

Saida shook hands with Callie and said, "You must be good at your job. Efraim is usually too negative about American policy to spend time with a government representative."

"He's coming around," Callie said. "I'm happy to meet you, Princess. The Secretary speaks highly of you."

"Are you based in Washington, D.C.?"

"Yes, but my roots are right here in Wind River County."

"It's such beautiful country," Saida said. "I'd love for you to show me around."

"You're not staying," Efraim said.

"That's not your decision," she said. "You don't have the authority to tell me what to do. You lost that opportunity when you refused to join in an arranged marriage with me. By the way, I thank you for that."

"An antiquated custom," he muttered.

No one had taken the idea of her marrying Efraim seriously, even though it would have knit their two countries more closely together. "I was only eleven at the time."

"You know, Saida, it wouldn't hurt for you to have a strong, powerful husband to fight your battles."

He might be dressed like an American cowboy, but his attitudes were old-school royalty. There was no point in arguing with him. He wouldn't change his mind.

Instead, Saida appealed to Callie. "Maybe you can make him understand. I'm not looking for a husband. And I won't run away and hide. I need to be here, searching for Amir."

"Actually," Callie said, "I have a solution that would work for both of you. Saida could go to Cheyenne—far enough away that she wouldn't be in danger but close enough to stay in touch with what's happening here."

"Why Cheyenne?" she asked.

"The Annual Cattlemen's Ball takes place there in a few days. A lot of people in the oil business attend, and I know they'd be honored to have the princess attend as a representative of the COIN nations."

"An excellent plan," Efraim pronounced. "If your brother was here, he would approve."

Unfortunately, he was correct. Amir was quick to shuttle her off to gala events where she could make contacts. "Thanks, Callie. I'll consider your suggestion. In the meantime, I have other concerns. The sheriff and I were just discussing my brother's disappearance. Could you brief me on—"

"Don't start," Efraim said as he stepped between them. "It's dangerous for you to be here, Saida. On the way here, we drove past the crime scene and saw the car you were driving. You could have been killed."

"Yes, there was a threat. However—as you can clearly see—I wasn't injured."

"A minor miracle," Efraim said.

"I can take care of myself," she insisted. "Tell him, Jake."

Until now, Jake had been standing back, watching their

argument through narrowed eyes. He spoke without smiling. "I saw part of the car chase. Saida walked away without injury because she's one hell of an amazing driver."

"Stay out of this," Efraim warned. "This is none of your business."

"But it is," Jake said. "The crime was committed in my county. On my watch."

"Of all people, you should know how dangerous it is for her to be here. You should want her to leave."

"Saida is a grown woman." Jake shifted his position in front of the mantle, squaring his shoulders to more directly confront Efraim. "She's capable of making her own decisions."

"The princess is under the protection of her brother. Since he isn't here, I will decide what's best for her. I won't allow her to put herself in danger."

She stepped forward. "I'm aware of the risk. I'd be a fool not to acknowledge the violence that has taken place here. And the deaths."

A shadow crossed Efraim's face, and she knew what he was thinking. She offered a condolence. "I'm sorry about Fahad."

"A traitor. I won't mourn his passing."

Easy to say, harder to accept. At one time, long ago, she'd had a minor crush on Fahad, the head of security for Efraim. His betrayal came after years of service.

"It's late," Efraim said as he turned on his heel and walked toward the door. "Come along, Saida. You'll stay at the resort tonight. Tomorrow, you'll return to California."

"No," she said firmly. She had to take a stand. "I won't leave until Amir is found. He's my brother, my blood, the only family I have left. I'll move mountains to find him. No obstacle is too great. No danger too intimidating. My only regret is that I didn't come here sooner. I will not leave."

A moment of silence followed her statement. Efraim regarded her thoughtfully. He wasn't accustomed to seeing such determination from her. Never mind that she'd built an independent life for herself in California, that she'd qualified for law school and earned excellent grades. He still saw her as Amir's annoying little sister whose only talent was to look pretty and smile.

Quietly, Jake said, "You're welcome to stay in my guest bedroom."

"I appreciate your hospitality."

Efraim's jaw tensed. He appeared to be on the verge of issuing a royal command until Callie touched his arm. "It appears to me," she said, "that this decision is made."

Efraim looked down at the woman beside him. When their eyes met, he softened, and then he sighed. "Very well."

Saida's inner self was high-kicking in a happy dance. Outwardly, she maintained her calm. "I'll be in touch."

Efraim nodded to Jake. "Keep her safe."

"That's my job."

JAKE HATED BULLIES. He always had.

Saida wasn't his idea of an underdog, but he didn't like the way Sheik Efraim had ordered her to leave town. Matter of fact, he didn't much like the sheik, at all. Tonight wasn't their first face-off and probably wouldn't be the last.

To be fair, Efraim's intentions toward Saida were good; he wanted to keep her safe. Jake had taken pretty much the same position, but he hadn't treated her like a moron and hadn't belittled her feelings for her brother.

He had empathy for Saida. When Efraim put her down, Jake's anti-bullying instincts kicked in. He'd been compelled to step in and offer his home as a refuge. Either he was really noble or really foolish. Whichever, the princess would be sleeping in his guest bedroom tonight.

After Efraim and Callie left, Jake arranged with Wheeler to have deputies guarding his house, front and back, on rotating shifts. He sent Wheeler off with a list of investigative tasks and priorities. First and foremost was to initiate the search for the black truck that crashed into Saida's car.

Entering the kitchen, he was hit with the smell of burnt cheese and garlic. His sister hovered over the counter and stared into a pan filled with a gooey, red blob. She poked at it with a spatula, and the blob crackled as though alive.

He glanced toward Saida who stood near the door with a water bottle in her hand. "Do I want to know what Maggie is doing?"

"It's my linguini." Maggie poked again and a hiss of steam exploded from the pan. "I left it warming in the oven too long. It's dead."

"Rest in peace," he said. "I would tell you to take the pan outside, but I don't want to poison the chipmunks."

She gestured with the spatula, flipping a bit of gooey red onto the adobe tiled floor. "I'd be mad at you for that comment if I wasn't so proud of you for letting Saida stay here tonight. You did the right thing."

Or not. "I have some ground rules, Saida."

"Of course."

Her eyes were wide and innocent as a baby kitten's. He reminded himself that she was more like a tigress. "Don't leave the house tonight. I have an alarm system and deputies posted outside so you ought to be safe."

"Fair enough."

"You can only stay here tonight. One night only." He couldn't spare the manpower to guard his house tomorrow while he was at work, and there was the possibility that the bad guys would come here looking for Saida. Maggie would be in danger. "When I leave for the office tomorrow, you're coming with me."

"What time?"

"Eight o'clock."

Though she nodded, her docile attitude was beginning to slip. "Tomorrow, I'll accompany you to your office. I'd like to review the crime reports."

"That's police business, not open to public scrutiny. Besides which, my department has been thorough. You won't find a lead that hasn't been pursued."

"He's right," Maggie said as she dumped the deceased linguini into a black garbage bag. "You shouldn't bother with the crime reports."

Since when was his baby sister the expert? "I suppose you have this all figured out."

"That's right." She wrapped the garbage bag tightly around the pan. "The best way for Saida to help with your investigation is to use what she knows about her brother, her family and the other COIN royals. I bet she's already told you stuff that nobody else knows."

He remembered Saida's story about her father, the former Sheik of Jamala, and his love of the West. There might be more relevant clues in her memory; his sister had a point. "All right. Good plan."

"Simple psychology," she said breezily.

"Works for me," the princess said. "I already have a few ideas about how to get started. I'll need to talk to some of the royal entourage, and then I can—"

"Stop." Jake reined her in before he lost control of the situation. He'd agreed to cooperate, but she wasn't running this show. "There's still the danger. You can't go running around, asking questions. Not without a bodyguard."

"Would it make a difference if I told you I had a gun?"

His empathy for her faded as his irritation kicked in. "How did you get a gun past airport security?"

"I came on a private jet, remember? And my weapons are

legal. They're both Beretta M9s, and I have concealed carry permits for California. Is there some sort of registration I need for Wyoming?"

He didn't want to snap at her, but he was beginning to understand Efraim's frustration in dealing with the princess. Sending her out in the world with a weapon might be the height of irresponsibility. "Do you know how to shoot?"

"I'm very accurate." She drew herself up as though insulted. "I learned marksmanship from Nasim, the same man who taught me evasive driving techniques."

Jake was beginning to piece a couple of things together. When he rescued her at the side of the road, she'd refused to leave her vehicle until she went through the suitcase in the backseat and found her makeup. But it wasn't mascara she wanted. She'd been after her Beretta M9. "You had your weapons in your luggage."

"Yes." Her gaze lowered, and she pretended interest in the toe of her shoe. The princess wasn't good at outright deception. Was she evasive? Yes. But she hadn't mastered the art of looking him in the eye and lying.

He asked, "What are you holding back?"

Without looking up, she said, "I packed six suitcases in a limited amount of time. I wasn't sure what I'd need when I got here, so I—"

"Saida," he interrupted. "Just tell me."

"I thought I'd packed both handguns, but when I looked in my suitcase a minute ago, I only found one."

"You're missing a gun. How is that possible?"

"When you dragged me away from the car, there was a time span before Wheeler got there. Probably fifteen or twenty minutes. Someone could have gone through my luggage."

Jake herded his sister and the princess into the front room

and pointed at the array of suitcases stacked beside the front door. He issued an order. "Search the luggage."

"All of it?" Saida asked.

He wasn't kidding around. "Make sure that your second gun isn't here. Is there someone you can call in Beverly Hills to see if you left the gun at home?"

"A housekeeper."

"Call her. I want all your weapons accounted for."

As he climbed the staircase to the second floor, he heard his sister cooing with delight. Obviously, Maggie was thrilled with the prospect of a fashion show.

In his master bedroom, Jake debated on whether he should leave the door open or closed. Though he had guards posted outside, he was still concerned. It would be just his luck to get into the shower at the same time Saida raised an alarm. His anger skipped a notch. Sharing a shower with the princess wouldn't exactly be the worst thing that could happen.

He sprawled backward across the bed. In spite of the caffeine he'd consumed less than an hour ago, he knew he'd be asleep in two winks if he closed his eyes. He forced his eyes to stay open as he stared at the ceiling.

What the hell was he going to do with the princess? For right now, he had the situation under control. But tomorrow?

He couldn't bring her to the office with him. Even before the royal crime spree hit Wind River County, he regularly put in a full day's work. Nor could Saida stay here at the house with Maggie. Sending her to the Wind River Ranch and Resort was the most logical option, but he didn't trust the so-called bodyguards in the royal entourage.

Another possibility occurred to him. Dragging himself off the bed, he went to the phone on his desk by the window and placed an international call.

Chapter Seven

Half an hour later when Jake went downstairs, his living room looked like a kaleidoscope had exploded. Colorful shoes, scarves, dresses, jackets and skirts draped over the furniture. Saida sat cross-legged on the floor with her Beretta in pieces in front of her on a newspaper. With slick efficiency, she reassembled her weapon and snapped in a fresh ammo clip.

This was another version of Saida—the warrior princess. Not a fashion icon, not a flirt, not a manipulator. In his opinion, this was her sexiest and most honest incarnation.

Clear-eyed, she met his gaze. "I'm missing a gun."

Later, he would ponder the implications. For right now, he simply accepted the fact. "Was anything else taken from your luggage?"

"Not that I can tell."

Maggie bounced toward him holding a bit of black lace in her hands. "Do you recognize this?"

"Tablecloth?"

"This is the original for a blouse I bought last year. Saida and I have the exact same taste. Do you believe it?"

"Great."

"Feel this." She rubbed a long, gray sheath against his cheek. "Is that the softest thing you've ever touched?"

He hadn't played dress-up with his sisters when they were kids and had no intention of starting now. "That's enough."

"And this scarf." Maggie uncoiled a long, silky scarf she'd wrapped around her neck. "Isn't it gorgeous? The pattern mirrors the Jamala crest. Red-and-gold with three horses running."

"Pack it up," he said. "Saida is leaving with me at eight in the morning, and she needs her luggage."

Saida scrambled to her feet. "What will we be doing?"

Since she was so damned anxious to investigate, he'd take advantage of her insights about her brother and her access to the insiders in the royal entourage. Until now, his dealings with the COIN princes hadn't been easy. These powerful men were accustomed to giving orders, not to answering interrogations. "I want you to start at the resort."

Disappointment flickered in her eyes. "Doing what?"

"Listening," he said. "They'll tell you a hundred times more than they'd ever reveal to an outsider."

"What do you need to know?"

"There's a big question that needs an answer," he said. "Why here? Out of all the places in the world he could choose, why did Amir arrange for the summit at the Wind River Ranch and Resort?"

"A coincidence?"

"According to Freud," Maggie said, "there are no coincidences. However, Jung had a different idea. He believed in this synchronicity thing."

"I'm with Freud on this." Jake couldn't believe those words had come from his mouth. "In any case, I think Amir had a reason for coming here."

Saida slipped her Beretta into the large side pocket of her shoulder bag. The gun fit so neatly that he suspected she'd had the purse specially designed to carry a concealed weapon. "Tell me more about what happened on the night he disappeared."

Jake considered stepping into the living room and taking a seat but decided against it. He didn't want to accidentally step on any of the super-soft, pretty clothes. "Amir gathered the COIN princes at the ranch, and then he left by himself, headed for a location he mentioned to no one else."

"A secret meeting," the princess said.

"Any ideas?"

"I have one," Maggie said. "Why don't you two go upstairs and talk about this stuff. I'll take care of the clothes."

"I wouldn't do that to you," Saida said. "It's my mess. I should clean up."

"It'll be my pleasure, believe me." Maggie shooed the princess toward the staircase. "Go ahead. You're going to have a busy day tomorrow. Get some sleep."

Jake assumed his baby sister was pushing her own match-making agenda by shoving him and Saida together, but he appreciated her help. It was hard to think when surrounded by clutter. "Thanks, Maggie."

He led the way up the staircase and made a left pivot into the guest room. Though his bedroom was considerably larger with a comfortable reading chair by the window and a desk, he didn't want to introduce the princess into his private lair. Resisting his attraction to her was hard enough; he didn't need the image of Saida in his bedroom imprinted on his brain.

Entering the bedroom, she slipped off her fur-collared vest. The fabric of the flesh-colored shirt hugged her curves. After she kicked off her boots, she sat at the head of the bed with her legs curled up beneath her. Her purple-tipped fingernails combed through her shiny, straight, black hair.

In an instant, she'd changed from a warrior to a soft, lovely woman. "Was it typical for Amir to arrange secret meetings?"

"He's not a sneaky person. When he was a teenager, he tried to teach me how to cover for him when he was dating two girls at the same time. His deception failed." She laughed. "Both girls found out and let him have it."

Though she wasn't doing anything to entice him, he felt a magnetic pull. If he let down his guard, he'd surely be drawn too close and do something he'd regret. He went to the window and checked to make sure the curtains were completely drawn. "Do you think Amir was meeting a woman?"

"Doubtful. Even if he's visited this area before, he never mentioned a girlfriend."

"Would he tell you?"

She gazed up and to the right while she considered his question. Her thoughtfulness impressed him. She could have snapped a quick answer, but she was taking the time to consider.

As he studied her, a wave of nervous energy surged through him. Did she know what kind of effect she had on men? Earlier, he would have said that she calculated every move. Now, he wasn't so sure.

Hoping to dissipate his tension, he paced from the window to the five-drawer pine dresser where he paused to smooth the fringe on a hand-woven runner that covered the top. His gaze bounced off the four walls. Had this room always been so small?

"My brother and I aren't close in the sense that we talk every day. Sometimes, weeks will pass without a word. But our connection is deep. If Amir went to the trouble of arranging a COIN summit at the Wind River Ranch and Resort so he could see a woman, she'd be important to him. I'm sure he'd mention her to me, but he said nothing."

"So we can rule out a girlfriend as his destination."

She nodded. "I believe so."

"Maybe his supposedly secret meeting didn't have any sort of significant meaning."

"How so?"

"With all due respect," he said, "your brother might have gone out looking for a hooker."

"Would that be likely? Is prostitution legal here?"

"Not anymore," he said. "Back in the gold rush days, Wyoming was famous for its bordellos. The town of Dumont was named for Eleanor Dumont, a famous madam and card shark."

A smile lit up her face. "Just like the cowboy movies with the saloon girls in fancy dresses. What did they call them? Soiled doves."

He wasn't about to take a trip into the Hollywood fantasy of the Old West where his people were usually portrayed as wild savages or comic relief sidekicks. "Keep the focus on Amir."

"I doubt he'd run off to see a hooker. It's not his style. Amir respects women, which is obvious when you think about how he treats me. He understands that I need to go to UCLA rather than to live the more cloistered life of a princess."

Rather than point out that she was different than most women, he stepped back. Forcing himself not to fidget, he leaned against the wall beside the door and hitched his thumbs in his belt. "Amir treats you as an equal."

"Not exactly." She exhaled a long sigh. "He still thinks of me as his baby sister. Like you and Maggie. You have two other sisters?"

"One is married and the other lives in Denver."

"You're the only male?"

"My dad's gone."

"I'm sorry for your loss."

"He's not dead." A familiar resentment prickled at the

edge of his memories. "He's an alcoholic, can't hold a job. He's been in and out of jail."

"I'm still sorry."

This conversation had veered into forbidden territory. His family history wasn't something he talked about. Not with anyone, certainly not with a princess.

There was nothing more he needed to say about his father. And yet, he was speaking. "Dad can't help who he is. Alcoholism is an illness, I know that. I want to help him. But I can't change him. No matter how hard I try. No matter how many times I talk to him or sign him in to rehab programs. It's his life, and there's only one thing I can do—accept him."

That might be the longest speech he'd ever made about his dad and their miserable relationship. If Maggie had been in the room, she would have been shocked, and then she would have given him a standing ovation. She was always saying that he needed to express his feelings. But he didn't feel any kind of relief.

Saida uncoiled her legs, rose from the bed and came toward him. "We can't choose our parents."

"Too bad." He shouldn't have opened up to her and revealed so much about himself, but it was done. As his mama always said, you can't unpeel an orange.

"Families are a test," she said. "They drive us crazy and make us proud. They teach us about anger and laughter. And love. Family is always at the core, at the heart."

"What does your heart tell you about Amir?"

"When I first heard that he was missing, it seemed unreal. I told myself that any minute, the phone would ring, and Amir would be laughing on the other end, telling me it was all a misunderstanding." She tossed her head, sending a ripple through her sleek, black hair. "I can't bear to lose my brother. If anything has happened to him…"

Though her voice broke, her features were composed, and

her caramel-colored eyes were dry. "We have to find him, Jake."

"I'm making you a promise." In all his years as a lawman, he had never done anything like this. One of the first rules of investigation is that you can't make iron-clad guarantees. Still, he continued, "Whatever it takes, I will find your brother."

"I believe you." Her posture was straight and proud, but her fingers trembled. She clenched her hands into fists and held them straight at her sides. The strain of worrying about her brother must be tearing her apart.

"Are you okay?" he asked.

"Fine," she said, too quickly.

"Saida, I know it's important for you to keep up a royal appearance, but there's nobody else around. I wouldn't tell a soul if you should happen to shed a tear."

"A princess isn't supposed to cry." As soon as she spoke, her eyes brimmed. It happened as fast as turning on a faucet. She covered her mouth, stifling a sob. "I'm sorry."

Jake knew he should keep his distance, but he couldn't ignore her suffering. He gathered her into his arms and held her quaking body, cradling her against his chest, protecting her from the storm of emotion that raged inside her. The only sound she made was the sharp intake of breath. Again and again, she gasped as she fought for control.

Her back bowed and her shoulders tensed. She leaned heavily against him as though she was unable to stand on her own. And he was glad to support her. His hands caressed her back, hoping to soothe her.

As quickly as her tears had appeared, she pulled herself together. With a determined gesture, she pushed away from him, her hands splayed on his chest.

Her chin lifted as she looked up at him. With his thumbs, he gently wiped away the moisture on her cheeks. It seemed like the most natural thing in the world to kiss her.

Chapter Eight

Saida gazed up into Jake's dark eyes and saw his concern, his kindness and his desire. His large hands gently cradled her face. His breath warmed her lips.

She wanted his kiss. She needed the comfort of a man's embrace. Jake made her feel safe.

Her right hand pressed against his chest, and she felt the beating of his heart, steady and strong. Her own pulse fluttered like a hummingbird. She closed her fingers, gripping his shirt below the collar and pulled him closer.

Her lips parted. Her eyelids closed. *Kiss me, Jake.* Breathless, she waited.

The pressure of his mouth against hers was firm and sweet, not at all sloppy. They shared a breath, an incredible intimacy. Excitement bubbled up inside her. She trembled, aware that this might be the best kiss she'd ever had in her entire life, not wanting this moment to end.

Too soon, he withdrew. His hands slipped from her face. As he separated from her, she snatched her hand from his chest.

Her eyes opened and met his. Both of them knew that kissing was inappropriate.

She hadn't intended to put him in this position, but when he'd spoken so candidly of his father, she'd been touched. From everything Maggie had told her, Jake wasn't a man who shared his emotions. The lone wolf. He didn't involve anyone else in his problems.

But he'd told her. For some reason, he'd trusted her.

And she'd done the same. Never before had she wept in front of a stranger. Public displays of emotions were not permitted. But she'd sobbed in Jake's arms.

"Tomorrow morning," he said.

"I'll be ready at eight o'clock."

She took a backward step as he left the room and closed the door. She and Jake were going to make a very good team.

THE NEXT MORNING, SAIDA dressed in her version of a no-nonsense detective's outfit—designer jeans, white shirt with a stand-up collar and gray linen jacket with black piping on the lapel. Her sensible, oxblood brogues were last season's fashion but very comfortable in case she needed to chase down a bad guy. Though she started off with no jewelry, she put on white gold hoop earrings and a black pearl necklace. Even a no-nonsense detective needs to accessorize.

There was a tap on the door and Maggie entered. "Hey, Saida. You look great."

"Will I fit in at your brother's office?"

"Not in a million years. Most of the women who work at the sheriff's department are older than dirt and think cable-knit cardigans are the height of fashion." She cocked her head to one side. "I thought you were going to be at the resort today?"

"To start with. But I'll be done quickly, and then I'll go to his office." She yanked her hair back from her face. "Should I wear it up or down?"

"Doesn't matter. Jake's ready to go. He sent me to get you."

The thought of seeing Jake started a pleasant quivering in her stomach. All night, she'd dreamed about that kiss. She'd analyzed that moment from every angle. He hadn't meant to kiss her, and the fact that it happened had to be kismet. Were they meant to be together? Was she making too much of one intimate gesture?

She hadn't come to Wyoming to kiss the sheriff. She was here to find her brother. "Wish me luck, Maggie."

Maggie gave her an impetuous hug. "You're going to do great."

Saida threw the last few items in her suitcase, zipped it and lugged it down the staircase where the rest of her luggage stood waiting. Jake strolled in from the kitchen as he ended a call on his cell phone.

He was wearing his dark blue uniform shirt with the sleeves rolled up—the same outfit he always wore when he did his daily press briefings. The first time she'd seen him on television, she'd noticed—as did probably every other red-blooded female who was watching—that he was a fine-looking man. In person, he was a thousand times more appealing.

"Perfect timing," he said.

As far as she was concerned, perfect was an accurate description for her bright, blooming optimism. "I promised to be ready by eight."

"It's eight-fifteen," he said, "but that's not a problem. We would have needed to wait anyway."

"For what?" A shadow slipped across her sunny state of mind.

"I made arrangements to keep you safe today, and it took an extra couple of minutes for everything to fall into place."

"Arrangements?"

The doorbell rang, and Jake answered.

Nasim stood framed in the doorway. In spite of the silver sprinkled through his wiry black hair, he was a formidable man. His stiff-necked military bearing made his navy sports jacket and turtleneck look like a uniform. His features had always reminded her of a hawk with sharp eyes and a hooked nose that bore a strong resemblance to a beak.

He gave her a nod which was his version of a bow. "My apologies, Princess Saida."

For destroying her plans? For inserting himself into a situation she'd rather handle herself? "Why?"

"I selected the wrong rental vehicle for you. The possibility of a high-speed chase did not occur to me."

Nasim had expected her to drive that boring little rental car to her lodgings and stay there, safely ensconced with the royal entourage. "Why are you here?"

"As soon as I heard what had happened, I perceived your need for a bodyguard." He looked toward Jake. "Sheriff Wolf contacted me last night while I was en route. He confirmed the possible danger. We are in agreement."

Jake reached out and shook his hand. "I'm glad you're here."

"No." She would not be shuttled off to the resort and kept out of the way. She hadn't come all the way to Wyoming to hide in an ivory tower. "I'm part of this investigation."

"No argument," Jake said. "I want your help, Saida. But you're in danger, and I can't provide the kind of full-time protection that you need."

Her hand rested on the front flap of her shoulder bag. In less than three seconds, she could draw her Beretta. In less than five, she could aim and shoot. Though she didn't regularly take target practice, she consistently had a high accuracy rating. "I can protect myself."

"This is true," Nasim said. "I trained you myself, and you are proficient. Nonetheless, the skills required to investigate are not physical."

"He's right," Jake said. "You're not going to be chasing down the bad guys with a high-powered rifle."

Nasim continued, "You need to concentrate your energy on mental acuity. Use your mind."

"I hate when you get all Yoda."

Unsmiling, Nasim did his Yoda impression. "Your mind, use you must."

Dealing with these two men was nothing like her confrontation with Efraim. Both Jake and Nasim believed in her and thought she was competent. But she was still angry. "You should have discussed this with me. Both of you."

When Jake rested his hand on her shoulder, a shimmer of electricity raced through her body, and she hated herself for responding to him. She didn't want to look at him, but she couldn't help herself.

"I'm not cutting you out," he said. "Nasim is here for security reasons. I still need you."

"When will we get together?"

"After I do the eleven o'clock briefing for the media. By then, I ought to have more information."

"What if you discover a significant clue before that?"

"I'll call you myself." He gave her shoulder a squeeze. "I promise."

He was an honorable man, and she had no choice but to believe him. "I still don't like this, but all right."

Nasim stepped aside to escort her through the door.

Parked outside was a giant yellow Hummer. Apparently, he was going for indestructible with this rental car.

INSTEAD OF THE ROOM THAT had been previously reserved for her, Saida moved into Amir's suite at the Wind River Ranch and Resort. It was ultraluxurious with two separate rooms, high ceilings, sitting areas with plush furniture and a king-size bed covered with fine Italian linens. A subtle blue silk-linen paper decorated the walls, and the carpet echoed that blue in a deeper shade.

Through the windows, she had a spectacular view of forested hillsides and a manicured lawn leading to green meadows. As she watched, two cowboys on horseback rode in the distance. Perhaps Amir had chosen this resort for no other reason than it was posh enough for the other princes and, at the same time, reminded him of the Old West stories their father told.

She pushed open French doors that led onto a patio with a breakfast area and a private hot tub. Very handy, she thought. The patio gave her another exit from the room.

Nasim supervised the unloading of her suitcases. Amir's clothing had already been packed away, and the closets were vacant. Later, she would call housekeeping to help her unpack. Right now, she had an investigation to get started.

Though she was supposed to be talking to the princes and uncovering their secrets, she wasn't anxious to repeat her experience with Efraim. She had a better idea for investigation, and it involved Danny Harold.

She sank into a blue-striped chair with a long view of the Wyoming countryside and signaled for Nasim to do the same.

"Lovely place," she said. "And there's a working ranch attached?"

"Several hundred head of cattle." He sat without relaxing his shoulders. His rigid spine barely touched the back of the chair. "They offer horseback riding and many other outdoor activities."

"I'm not interested in any of those things," she said. "I'm here to take an active role in searching for my brother."

"And I will assist you," he said. "I'm concerned about Amir. His absence has left a power vacuum in Jamala."

That wasn't the only reason. Even though he was more of a role model than their biological father, Nasim would never admit that he loved her and her brother as much as his own kids. But she knew. "I'm going to start my investigating by calling someone, and I need to meet with him alone."

"The suite has two rooms," he pointed out. "You can meet in the outer area. I will stay out of sight."

"Two rooms but only one bed." She took out her cell phone. "Where will you sleep tonight?"

"Until the men who threatened you are apprehended, I will not close my eyes."

Oh, swell. She knew better than to argue with this stubborn old man. He'd flown halfway around the world to keep an eye on her and would not be dissuaded from his task. "I hope you got some sleep on the plane."

"Your security is my only concern." He stroked his chin and tilted his head to one side—a gesture that meant he was thinking.

"Something else?" she asked.

"There is someone else I would trust to keep you safe, Princess," he said. "Sheriff Jake Wolf. A good man."

She hadn't expected that judgment. Nasim didn't give his trust lightly. "Do you like Jake because he called on you to help?"

"A wise decision." Nasim nodded.

She called the number on Danny Harold's card and told him what she needed. Within a half hour, he was escorted to her room by the scowling head of security. After the security man introduced himself, he asked if she would inform him when her guest was ready to leave. He explained, "In light of all that's happened we're trying to limit the number of unauthorized people in the hotel."

"Understandable," she said. "Thank you."

Danny sniffed around her sitting room like a stray dog and touched everything from the hand-carved mantel above the fireplace to the fresh flower arrangement on the side table.

"Classy, real classy. I could get used to living in places like this."

She glanced toward the closed bedroom door where Nasim was resting. If he came crashing into the room, he might spook Danny. She kept her voice low so she wouldn't wake her self-appointed bodyguard. "Did you bring the photos?"

"Right here." He patted the large camera bag he carried on a strap slung over his shoulder. "Memory cards for all the pictures I've taken since I got to Wyoming. I've got dozens of shots of the princes."

"And the crowds?" Photos of royalty didn't interest her; she hoped to find suspicious individuals among those who had gathered.

Proudly, Danny said, "I've got it all. Even a couple of landscapes."

She seated herself in a chair to the right of the polished cherry coffee table and opened her laptop. "I'd like to see them."

"Not so fast." He plunked himself down in the center of the sofa. "What's in it for me?"

Saida had known that she'd need to barter with Danny; he was the sort of man who kept score. "I have a proposition."

"Wow." His eyes popped wide, and then he leered. "If you're going to offer what I think you're going to offer, my answer is *yes, ma'am.*"

"What are you talking about?"

"Come on, Saida. You know there's chemistry between us. Am I right?"

Of course, he'd jump to the most obnoxious conclusion. As if she'd trade sexual favors for his pictures? After all these years of stalking her, he ought to understand that she would never sell herself so cheaply. In fact, never at all. "You insult me."

"On the contrary, princess. You're a desirable woman, and I'm a—"

"Listen to me, Danny Harold." Her voice was ice-cold. "In exchange for your photos, I will hire you to take my official portrait."

"What's that mean?"

"I would be garbed in traditional clothing and royal jewels. If the portrait is satisfactory, it would hang in the palace in Jamala. Of course, you would be well paid for your work. But the real value is the honor of being chosen."

"Yeah, I can't take honor to the bank," he muttered.

"I would recommend you to other royal families. This could be the start of a new career for you."

Danny transformed from lustful to greedy. Dollar signs flashed in his eyes as he imagined traveling from palace to palace as the royal photographer.

"You got a deal." He flipped open his camera bag. "I can load these memory cards into your laptop right now."

Her investigation was underway.

Chapter Nine

Jake stood at the window of his office on the second floor of the Wind River County Courthouse in Dumont. In ten minutes, he had his morning media briefing on the front stairs outside, and the crowd had already assembled. Television vans lined the street. Reporters with microphones, cameramen, photographers and paparazzi were waiting for him. Sheriff Jake Wolf was slated to be the guest of honor at a party he didn't want to attend.

There were more of them than yesterday. Saida's arrival had fired up interest. Though she had less actual power than any of the other COIN royals, she was the most famous.

His office wasn't big enough to pace back and forth, but Jake felt the need to move around. Physical activity helped jog his brain, and he needed to be careful about how much he revealed to the reporters.

Seated behind his desk, he picked up a cantaloupe-size basketball. Juggling the ball from hand to hand, he eyeballed the hoop mounted opposite his desk chair. When this office had belonged to Burt Maddox, that wall had been packed with framed certificates, awards, diplomas and photos of the former sheriff with important people, including a snapshot of Maddox and Dick Cheney on a hunting trip.

His highly placed connections had saved him from criminal prosecution. Maddox had been suspected of dirty dealings that ranged from taking bribes to blocking criminal investigations that would have damaged the reputations of his supposedly important friends. Though Jake would have loved to see Maddox in jail, the district attorney didn't want to open that can of worms. It was enough to have Big Burt out of office and retired to his horse farm on the outskirts of town.

Recently, there had been rumblings from people who wanted Maddox back in office. They accused Jake of incompetence and questioned his abilities. The COIN crime spree was tearing his county apart and focusing a negative spotlight on Wind River.

He tossed the basketball in a neat arc. It bounced off the rim. A miss. Damn. There was a lot he was missing.

Forensics had found fingerprints on Saida's vehicle, but AFIS turned up no matches. Wheeler had talked to the crew at the private airfield and had come up empty. Right now, the deputy was tracking down leads on the possibility of the sedan being a rental.

As Jake left his chair to pick up the ball, he looked through the half-glass wall that separated his office from the other desks and file cabinets that made up the sheriff's department. Deputy Wheeler came around the front counter and made a beeline for Jake's open door.

In spite of his long hours of overtime, Wheeler looked sharp in his uniform shirt and slacks. He yanked off his cowboy hat as he stuck his head into Jake's office. "Sheriff, I've got a suspect. His name is William Dormund, and he's from Cheyenne. Yesterday afternoon at approximately five o'clock, he rented a black four-door sedan at the airport."

"How do we know this is the car that chased the princess?"

"I checked with every single one of the car rentals. Dormund's car was the only one that fit our description. He rented it for the whole week and said he'd return the car when he got back home to Cheyenne."

It was the closest they'd come to a suspect. "You have the license plate number?"

Wheeler nodded. "I already put out an APB."

"Good work." He clapped his deputy on the shoulder. "Dig up all the information you can on William Dormund. Use Jane Cameron and her forensic computer geniuses."

"And the FBI?"

"Let's not inform them yet. We should make sure Dormund is our guy before we call in the big dogs." Jake picked up the phone on his desk. "I need to make one call, and then I've got to talk to the gang downstairs. I want you with me for the briefing."

"How come?"

"You're looking all neat and official in your uniform. You're a fine representative of this department."

"Thanks, Jake."

As Wheeler stepped outside, Jake punched in the number for Saida's cell phone. He'd only talked to her once this morning when she told him she'd been going through all the photos her paparazzo friend had taken and had found a couple of people who turned up in photos taken at different times.

After the press briefing, he intended to go to the resort and take a look at those pictures. But getting her input on this new lead was important.

She greeted him with a burst of excitement. "I'm so glad you called."

On the phone, he noticed the lilt of her slight accent. "Why's that?"

"I found a theme in Danny's photos. Everybody is falling in love."

"What?"

"Last night at your house, it was clear that something was

going on between Efraim and Callie. And it appears that the other COIN princes have coupled up. It's a bit unusual, to say the least. Anyway, I've been doing some prowling around and—"

"You haven't left your room, have you?"

"Nasim is always with me," she said. "And we're driving in a bulletproof vehicle. We're fine. No problems."

Though he would have preferred to keep her under house arrest, there was no way to cage this princess. Jake tried not to think of her and Nasim racing around the back roads and terrorizing the cattle in their yellow Hummer.

"We have a lead," he said. "There's reason to believe that the man driving the sedan was William Dormund. Does that name mean anything to you?"

She repeated the name a few times. "Sorry, Jake. I can't place him, and I'm very good at remembering things like that. Recognizing people is part of my diplomatic training."

With her background, she'd probably handle the media better than he did. Right now, he should be on his way downstairs to meet them. But he didn't want to hang up. "I have to do the media briefing."

"I'll be watching you," she said. "I found an internet connection that broadcasts your press conference live."

Just what he needed. More attention on crime in Wind River County. "As soon as I'm done, I'll come to the resort."

"I'll be waiting for you. Good luck."

He placed the receiver back onto the cradle, stood and took another shot with his mini-basketball. It swished through the hoop and landed with a thud in the circular wastebasket below. Talking to the princess had improved his aim.

She seemed to make everything better. He'd tried to put their inappropriate kiss out of his mind, but he couldn't forget what that moment felt like. He'd had a sense that his world had changed, that she'd made a difference.

He held on to that feeling of well-being as he and Wheeler descended the staircase to the first floor. Other people with offices in the courthouse offered greetings which he returned without slowing down to chat. He wanted to get this briefing over with.

Outside, the day was sunny, and there was enough wind to ruffle the American flag on the pole. Jake moved into position at the top of the concrete steps. During the course of this investigation, he'd become acquainted with most of these reporters and photographers, so he noticed a new face—a woman with over-whitened teeth set off by shiny, blood-red lipstick. She brandished her microphone like a club.

"Good morning," Jake said. "As most of you know, Princess Saida Khalid of Jamala has come to Wind River County. She's deeply concerned about her brother, Sheik Amir Khalid. We're following all leads and hope to resolve the case soon."

Lipstick elbowed her way to the front of the pack. "Is it true that Princess Saida spent last night at your house?"

Not something he intended to discuss. "Next question?"

"I want an answer, Sheriff." When Lipstick opened her mouth, she looked like she wanted to take a bite out of him. "You're not married, are you? Did she stay at your place?"

The suggestion of improper behavior was too blatant to ignore. "Last night," he said, "for her own protection, Princess Saida stayed in the guest bedroom at my house where I live with my sister. Two deputies stood guard outside."

Someone else asked, "Is she in danger?"

"In light of threats to all the COIN royals, we're taking every precaution." In case the men who tried to abduct her were listening, he added, "She is now being protected by her own bodyguard from Jamala who arrived this morning."

Lipstick jabbed her microphone at him. "Is he better than you at protecting her?"

"I wouldn't cross him," Jake said.

A reporter who had been attending press conferences since the beginning called out, "I heard that Princess Saida was involved in a car accident."

Jake exhaled a brief, frustrated sigh. Though he'd hoped to avoid a big drama, he'd expected information about the attempted abduction to be leaked. Too many people knew. Too many were willing to talk about how incompetent the sheriff's department was. The princess had been in town for only a few hours and had already been in danger. Where was he while Saida was being attacked? How had he allowed this to happen?

The best damage control was to downplay the attack and keep it from turning into a headline. "Yes," he said, "there was a car accident."

"A high-speed chase?" the reporter asked.

Jake leveled with them. "While Princess Saida was driving herself to the Wind River Ranch and Resort, she was forced off the road by two other vehicles. She wasn't hurt."

A ripple of excitement chased through the crowd. They were on the scent of a real story. Questions flew like hailstones: What happened to the other cars? Do you have suspects? How did she escape?

Jake raised a hand, signaling for quiet. When the commotion faded to a dull roar, he said, "Nothing to report right now. I'll keep you apprised of further developments."

"Hey, Jake." A familiar and deeply irritating voice boomed his name. "I got a piece of information that just might help you out."

Burt Maddox swaggered toward him. He wasn't nicknamed "Big Burt" because of his height. At six feet two inches, Jake was considerably taller. But Maddox was built like a refrigerator. The pearl snaps on his fancy embroidered cowboy shirt strained to the breaking point. When he accidentally-on-purpose nudged Jake's shoulder, it took an effort not to be knocked over.

Arms raised like a conquering hero, Maddox waved to the media. "Howdy, folks. In case you don't know, I was sheriff in these parts for fifteen years. I'm retired now, but I like to keep track of what's going on."

The locals recognized the former sheriff. Whether they loved him or hated him, the reporters were glad to see him. Maddox was flamboyant. He always gave them a story.

From Jake's perspective, Maddox was trouble. He wanted to get this jerk out of here as quickly as possible. Stifling a gag reflex, he shook hands. "I appreciate any help you can give us, Burt. Let's step inside and talk."

"A little birdie told me you were on the lookout for a couple of vehicles," Maddox said.

Jake had already mentioned two cars that forced Saida off the road. "We have leads and we're—"

"I've already located one of the vehicles," Maddox announced as he beamed for the cameras. "That's right. Crime solved."

He paused, waiting for applause that didn't happen, and then he continued, "You all might wonder how I figured this out while Jake was sitting on his thumbs. Well, here's the deal. Being a sheriff is a whole lot more than following proper procedures. You've got to know the territory, to be familiar with the folks in your jurisdiction. Everybody in these parts knows Big Burt Maddox."

Obviously, he was grandstanding. Did he have actual information or was he taking advantage of a press conference to make Jake look bad? He glanced over at Wheeler who responded with a confused shrug.

A local reporter called out, "Where's the car, Burt?"

Jake flashed on visions of a media mob swarming his crime scene, destroying evidence. He got a grip on Maddox's fleshy upper arm and turned him away from the microphones. "Don't give the location. You know what will happen."

"That's your problem, Sheriff Wolf." He spoke Jake's name with a sneer. "Take your hand off me."

"Be reasonable."

"Go to hell, Jake."

He wrenched away and spun around to face his audience with a broad grin. "Ever since this stuff started happening with these fancy-pants royal folks, I've been thinking. They aren't in danger from any of us locals. There's no reason for any citizen of Wind River County to give a hoot about their countries, excepting that we hate being gouged by oil-rich foreigners."

Lipstick was the only person who kept her focus trained on Jake. "Is that how you feel, Sheriff? Do you hate the sheiks?"

"No." Jake was too appalled by her question to say more.

"What about Princess Saida?" Lipstick called out. "How do you feel about her?"

Clearly, he had lost control of the situation. His fingers clenched into fists. If he punched Maddox in the gut, it might ruin his standing and reputation. But it might be worth it.

"Well, now," Maddox said, "you can talk to Jake about his crush on the princess after I get done solving his case for him."

"Yeah," said a local, "let Big Burt finish what he has to say."

Maddox said, "I figured that if locals were mixed up in this mess, they had to be getting paid off. Some bad guy with deep pockets had come to town and was hiring people to do his bidding. That's when I noticed Chad Granger was spreading money around."

Jake knew Chad Granger, knew where he lived, knew that he owned a truck. If he and Wheeler moved fast, they might be able to reach Granger's place before the camera crews. He turned to his deputy. "Is your car close?"

"Yessir."

Jake stepped up to the microphones. "We're done. Next briefing is four o'clock."

As he and Wheeler walked away, he heard Maddox start in. "No need for you folks to leave. Based on my years of experience, I'd be happy to give my theory of how the current situation…"

Jake kept on walking. *Die, blowhard.*

Chapter Ten

In the passenger seat of the Hummer with her laptop perched on the console, Saida had watched Jake's press conference with dismay. His opening words had been just fine. He'd presented a very sherifflike image of responsibility and control. And, of course, gorgeousness.

The camera loved Jake. His shoulders seemed impossibly broad, yet still in proportion with his narrow hips. Sunlight glistened in his black hair. His deep-set eyes, high cheekbones and strong jaw made him rugged. She would have been happier if the live feed on her computer had begun and ended with a simple picture of Jake standing in front of the courthouse.

Unfortunately, that hadn't happened. Right away he'd been hit with the question about why she'd stayed at his house, and he'd struggled to avoid the taint of scandal. Poor Jake!

If she'd been at the briefing, she could have easily defused that reporter. For years, she'd been dealing with nasty insinuations about her personal life, which she counted as one of the reasons she'd never had a relationship that lasted for more than a couple of months.

Jake's problems had gotten worse when that horrible Maddox person had popped up with his snide references about Jake's incompetence and his assertion that he'd found the truck. Was it true? Had this buffoon stumbled across a legitimate clue?

When Jake left the press conference, she knew he was going to check on that lead. And she wanted to be there.

"Nasim," she called out the open window. "We need to go."

He came around the front of the vehicle to her window. The parking place he'd chosen was a pull-off in a grassy field beside a barbed-wire fence with unrestricted views in all directions. She supposed Nasim had a strategic reason for selecting this particular spot but hadn't asked.

He rested his arm on her window ledge. "What is our destination?"

"The truck that ran me off the road might have been found."

A pained expression pinched his lips. "Again, I apologize for the puny rental car. I should have realized that—"

"Nasim," she interrupted, "you take better care of me than anyone else possibly could. Your service to my family has always been above and beyond."

"The family is in disarray." His expression darkened. "You were threatened. Amir is missing."

"Which is why we need to get moving."

While they drove, she continued to watch the press conference on her computer screen. The bulky, unpleasant Maddox clearly enjoyed the spotlight. He postured and carried on, ignoring questions about where he had seen the damaged truck. His reluctance to reveal that information was the responsible thing to do. If he mentioned the site, the media would go charging off in that direction and cause trouble.

Jake had seemed to know where he was headed. To the home of the truck's owner, Chad Granger? It wouldn't be difficult for her to look up the address and follow the GPS instructions. But what if the truck wasn't at Granger's house?

As if in reply to her silent question, Maddox said, "I

keep an eye on my neighbors. When I checked around Chad Granger's place, I saw what I needed to see."

Aloud, she said, "The truck is at the home of Chad Granger."

After a moment's search and scan, she and Nasim had their coordinates. As they drove, she told him about Maddox and the press conference.

Nasim tapped the side of his prominent nose. "Something smells fishy."

"How so?"

"Mr. Maddox is an enemy of Sheriff Wolf. By finding this important clue, he creates embarrassment for the sheriff. I think, perhaps, this discovery is too convenient."

She appreciated the way Nasim thought. "You're suggesting that Maddox knew about the truck because he and Granger are working together."

Again, he tapped his nose. "Fishy."

But why would Maddox betray his partner?

She leaned back in the comfortable seat and stared through the windshield of the Hummer. The wide, open Wyoming landscape became a bit more populated as they passed a crossroads with a cluster of motorcycles, a bar and a gas station. The houses were acres apart. Many had been abandoned; the wood structures weathered to a ghostly gray.

"I must ask," Nasim said, "will we be helping Sheriff Wolf in his investigation? Or will our presence be a nuisance?"

"Definitely a help." On this point, she was crystal clear. "There are some things I can do better than he can."

"I see." Nasim made a snorting noise that resonated in his nose and came out as a honk. "The sheriff will be most fortunate to have your assistance."

JAKE HAD ONLY BEEN SHERIFF for a year, but he'd paid his dues as a cop and a detective. His police experience told him that rushing from the courthouse to Granger's property was a mistake. He didn't have a warrant, didn't even have his gun or handcuffs. He was unprepared, unprofessional.

But he had no choice. He and Wheeler had to move fast. If Granger knew he'd been identified as the owner of the truck, he'd turn rabbit and run.

Using the police radio in Wheeler's SUV, he called for all available units to respond to Chad Granger's house. Jane Cameron and her forensic team wouldn't be needed unless they actually found the damned truck.

He asked Wheeler, "Do you have an extra gun?"

Wheeler took his eyes off the road for a second to look at him. "No, sir."

When Jake had been working the city beat in Cheyenne, he carried a sidearm, wore an ankle holster and had an additional weapon in his car. The pace of crime in Wind River County was considerably slower. "I'll take your stun gun. How about vests?"

"Two in the back. Do you think we'll need them?"

"If Maddox was telling the truth, Granger was getting paid to cause trouble for the royals. He could be involved in some of the other violence." Those attacks ranged from sniper fire to bombs. "We'll treat Granger as an armed and dangerous suspect."

"You're the boss." Wheeler's cheeks flushed red. This might be the most excitement he'd ever encountered on the job. "What do we do when we get there?"

"Put on the vests. Approach the house with weapons drawn. If Granger doesn't answer, we'll take a quick look around. There's no need to bust down his front door."

Not without a warrant or a solid reason to suspect that Granger was a danger to himself or others. The tip from Maddox might turn out to be nothing. Jake wouldn't be surprised; this whole thing felt like a setup.

They were nearing the long driveway leading to the ramshackle ranch that belonged to Chad Granger. "Turn off the lightbar," Jake said. "On the off chance that he doesn't know we're coming for him, let's not give him an alert."

The big white SUV with the sheriff's logo on the side was warning enough. Wheeler slowed as he made the final turn.

"Granger has let this place go to hell," Wheeler said. "Before his mama died, it used to be neat and pretty."

Not anymore. Weeds consumed the garden plot. The paint on the little two-story was cracked and peeling. A scrap of cardboard was duct taped over a broken window. The barn behind the house was even more disreputable—not fit for livestock, not even sheep.

"I never knew the late Mrs. Granger," Jake said. His prior visits to this house had been to arrest or to question Chad—a stupid, mean drunk who was prone to fistfights.

"A decent lady," Wheeler said, "she played organ at the church and gave piano lessons. After her husband died, she struggled to make ends meet."

Jake remembered Saida saying that we can't choose our parents. The opposite was also true. The churchgoing Mrs. Granger would have been sorely disappointed in her son.

Ironically, Saida's arrival in town and the botched abduction attempt might provide the best lead he'd had on solving the royal crime spree. If Granger was actually involved, it wouldn't be hard to convince this weak-minded moron to give up his connections for a lesser sentence.

Wheeler parked. They put on the vests and mounted the steps to the long porch, which was littered with rusting beer cans. A mangy black cat slipped around the edge of the house and hopped onto an overturned rocking chair to watch.

Jake hammered on the door. "Sheriff's department. Open up, Granger."

He stepped to one side in case Granger decided to shoot

through the door. Wheeler stood opposite with his gun held in both hands, ready to shoot. They listened hard. No sound came from inside the house. Jake knocked twice more.

"If he's in there," Wheeler said, "he's not moving around."

Jake stepped off the porch. "Let's take a quick look around."

He hoped they'd find something that would justify breaking into Granger's house. The garage door was open. Inside, Jake saw a shiny, new motorcycle. "I wouldn't think Granger could afford this machine."

"Maddox said he was throwing money around. I guess this is proof."

"Makes sense," Jake said. But even a scumbag like Granger might have come into unexpected money. "It's not enough. We need evidence that will stand up in court."

The black cat crossed their path and headed toward the barn, which was probably its natural habitat—a veritable sanctuary for field mice. Jake followed.

On the far side of the barn, he found the truck. Like the rest of Granger's property, the vehicle was filthy. The passenger side was badly scraped and dented.

"Here's your proof," Wheeler said.

Jake circled the truck being careful not to touch anything and leave prints. He peered over the edge into the truck bed and saw an array of clutter: an old tire, beer cans, two unopened bags of cement. A pile of old, filthy blankets and drop cloths were arranged at one side of the bed.

Wheeler held out a pair of white latex gloves. "The CSIs will have my butt if we don't put these on."

"That's good police work. Professional." Unlike Jake who had bolted from the press conference, his deputy was prepared for whatever they might find. Irritated with himself, Jake stuck his fingers into the gloves. "I want to see what's under those blankets."

He lowered the back gate and climbed onto the truck bed. From this angle, it was obvious that the blankets were covering something. He lifted the edge of one blanket. There was a stink, the smell of blood and excrement. He saw a partially clenched fist. The flesh was pale, so white it was almost blue.

The top blanket might have been beige at one time but was so covered by grit and oil stains that the color was indecipherable. The next covering was a drop cloth that had been used for painting. Jake pulled it back.

The body lay flat on his back with his arms at his sides. His eyes stared blindly into the sky. His forehead was a bloody pulp. Jake reckoned it was an exit wound. The killer had put a gun to the back of his head, pulled the trigger and blown away half the skull.

He hunkered down beside the dead man and tried to bend his arm. Full rigor had set in. He'd been killed over twelve hours ago. After the chase with Saida.

Wheeler peered over his shoulder. "That's not Granger."

"This man is wearing a suit. I doubt Granger owns anything this nice."

Wheeler stepped back so fast that the truck jolted. He pivoted, averting his gaze. It was hard for Jake to believe that his deputy was squeamish. Wheeler was an avid hunter who shot and field-dressed his kills.

"Are you okay?" Jake asked.

"The smell. It's getting to me."

The murder affected Jake, too. Though he was sheriff, he was still a man—an Arapaho with a connection to Mother Earth and all her creatures. A dark chill sank into his skin. Later, he would cleanse his spirit.

To Wheeler, he said, "I need for you to keep an eye on the house. Make sure Granger doesn't take this opportunity to sneak away. Don't enter until I join you."

"Yes, sir."

Jake took out his cell phone and put through a call to the chief forensic investigator, Jane Cameron. "I'm at Chad Granger's house. We found the truck."

"Maddox was right," Jane said darkly. "I hate when that happens."

"It gets worse. There's a body."

"Granger?"

"I don't recognize him," Jake said. "Looks like he was shot in the back of the head."

"Like a gangland execution. I didn't know we had a Mafia problem in Wind River County." She gave a short, nervous laugh. "I'll notify the coroner and get there as fast as I can."

"Here's the deal, Jane. I know I shouldn't touch the body until after you and the coroner are done, but I've got to act fast on this." The coroner was notorious for taking hours to respond to a call. "I'm going through his pockets to see if he has ID."

"Do whatever you need," she said. "I'm on my way."

After he disconnected the call, he reached into the inner jacket pocket with his gloved hand. Inside, he found an envelope containing a boarding pass for a flight from Cheyenne to Dumont and a receipt for a rental car, both made out to the same name. The victim was William Dormand, the guy who'd rented the sedan.

As Jake was about to stand, he noticed a bright shimmer on the truck bed near the victim's shoulder. He picked up a round earring no bigger than a dime. Black enamel with crossed swords, it matched the ring Saida was wearing last night.

Chapter Eleven

Jake knew better than to tamper with evidence. He shouldn't have touched the earring, should have left it for Jane Cameron and the forensic investigators to find.

Why was Saida's earring left here? This murder scene had been staged with the body laid out on his back and covered where they'd be sure to find him. Was the earring supposed to be a threat, a reminder that she was still in danger? Or was this shiny bit of evidence supposed to implicate the princess in this murder?

Either way, he didn't want Saida dragged any deeper into this miasma. Her motive for coming here was pure; all she wanted was to find her brother.

Jake stuffed the earring into his pocket. There was no justification for hiding evidence, but he'd made his choice. Saida's well-being was more important than the law.

As he strode toward the front of the house to join Wheeler, he spotted a vehicle coming down the driveway. A big, fat, yellow Hummer.

Saida was here.

The massive car parked, and Nasim emerged from the driver's side. Through the windshield, Jake saw the princess. She gave a cheerful wave as though they were meeting for a party instead of storming the house of a suspect.

Nasim approached. "Can I be of service?"

"I assume you're armed," Jake said.

He nodded.

Jake also assumed that Nasim was an expert marksman who could shoot the wings off a gnat. Not a bad person to provide backup.

"Draw your weapon. We're searching the house." Jake glanced over his shoulder toward the Hummer. "What about Saida?"

"I have advised her to stay in the car."

Which didn't mean she'd obey. If Granger actually was in the house and tied to pull something, Jake didn't want the princess in the line of fire. He went toward the Hummer.

She lowered the window. "Is the truck here?"

"That's right," he said. "Don't leave the car until I give you the okay."

"I understand." She handed her Beretta through the window. "This might be more effective than your cute little stun gun."

He shouldn't be grinning at her, but he couldn't help himself. "Thanks."

At the front door, Jake didn't waste time by knocking. "We'll search the house. Wheeler, take the upstairs. Nasim and I will cover the downstairs. I'll go left."

Before kicking down the door, he tried the knob. It turned easily in his hand. Granger hadn't even bothered locking up. Not a good sign. He'd probably fled hours ago.

The three of them rushed through the house, checking corners and closets. Jake's initial assumption was confirmed: nobody home.

The kitchen was particularly disgusting with a sink full of dirty dishes, pots and pans. The table was piled high with papers and mail. Buried in this mess might be a clue to where Granger had gone.

To Wheeler he said, "Since Granger couldn't take his truck

and didn't use the motorcycle, he must have another vehicle. See if there's anything registered to him, get the license plates and put out an APB."

"Got it."

With Nasim, Jake walked toward the Hummer. "Thanks for your help."

"I wish we had found the driver." Nasim's tone suggested that he would have shot first and asked questions later.

"How did you and Saida get here so quickly?"

"Princess Saida observed the press conference. She found the address of Chad Granger and used the GPS. We were already in the Hummer."

"Any reason you and Saida decided to leave the resort?"

"The princess entertains definite ideas. She preferred to avoid Efraim and the other princes."

Which was the exact opposite of what he'd asked her to do. She was supposed to be gathering inside info about COIN. When they were in sight of the Hummer, Jake motioned to her that she could come out.

With zero hesitation, she responded, rushing toward him. As he watched her approach, he forgot for a moment that he was in the midst of a difficult investigation. The tension knotting his muscles loosened when she flashed her smile.

He heard the sound of sirens as his other deputies drew near. "You and Nasim should go back to the resort. I'm going to be busy here for a while."

"I can help," she said. "In fact, I insist that you let me take care of this one thing."

"What thing is that?" Enthusiasm was one thing; expertise was another.

"The media." She spread both hands palms up as if offering him a solution. "It only took me a couple of minutes to figure out where Chad Granger lived. I'm pretty sure the TV vans are already on their way."

After this morning's press conference, Jake wasn't looking forward to another go-round with reporters, especially not with Ms. Lipstick. The murder had added another layer of complexity to the situation. He couldn't shove this responsibility onto Saida's slender shoulders.

"Much as I'd like to take you up on the offer," he said, "I can't appoint you spokesperson for the sheriff's department."

"I wouldn't speak in an official capacity. I promise not to talk about anything pertaining to the investigation."

He liked that idea. "That might work."

"I'll park the Hummer at the road leading to the house. Give me one deputy who can control who enters, and I'll handle everything else until you're ready to make an official statement."

Why the hell not? "You're on, Princess."

AFTER SAIDA GOT HERSELF situated at the end of the long driveway leading to Granger's house, she prepared to meet the media. Her conservative outfit wasn't exactly right. Though she intended to be serious, people with cameras expected a bit of flash and dazzle from a princess.

She left her jacket in the Hummer. Her high-collared blouse was sleeveless and white with pleating at the front—simple and sophisticated but not colorful enough for television. She repurposed her black pearl necklace by double-looping it around her wrist as a bracelet, and she used a red-and-gold silk scarf that she had in her purse as an ascot. Her Beretta would have made an interesting accessory, but she was here to defuse rumors and to protect Jake from the negative impression that might have been left by the earlier press conference.

Leaning against the hood of the Hummer with Nasim standing nearby, she waited while the television van from

Channel Six was turned back by the deputy posted at the driveway.

The van parked at the side of the road, and the reporter bounded toward her. "You're the princess, right?"

"Yes." Though she withheld her smile, she gave him an encouraging nod.

The reporter—a blue-eyed man with floppy brown hair—introduced himself and asked if he could interview her. He was probably the same age as Saida, but she had decades on him in terms of experience. Deftly, she manipulated their positions so the sun wouldn't be shining directly in her eyes. When the cameraman set up his tripod, he could contain both of them in a single shot with the mountains in the background.

Saida explained her presence by saying that she was waiting to speak with the sheriff. The only information she had that pertained to the investigation was that the little house at the end of the driveway belonged to Chad Granger, and the sheriff had found a truck that might have been the one that tried to run her off the road.

As she spoke and answered questions, she subtly flirted with the youthful reporter, offering a degree of warmth while avoiding any blatant suggestion of sexuality. Persuasion came in many forms, and she'd practiced this skill, wielded it like a weapon.

The reporter was hooked. He leaned toward her. His voice lowered. His pupils dilated. He showed all the signs of a man who was interested in her as a woman.

Another reporter and cameraman joined the first, then another. She worked her magic, used her power as she spoke of Jamala—the beaches and palm trees and the warm Mediterranean. Her homeland, though different from the high plains of Wyoming and the mountain ranges, shared a common interest in oil.

Nothing she said would make headlines, but the group that gathered around her was interested and encouraging. They wanted to hear more from her, wanted to be with her.

Saida knew that she was an attractive woman. Certainly, she had flaws. Who didn't? But she was blessed with regular features, a healthy body and the good taste to dress well.

Her flirting also worked with women. The aggressive female reporter with harridan-red lipstick demanded to know about her relationship with the sheriff. "What's going on, Princess Saida? You spent the night at his house."

"I'm sure you understand." Saida reached toward her, welcoming her into a special circle of friendship. "After I survived the high-speed chase, I was shaken. Sheriff Wolf was kind enough to offer his protection."

The woman smirked. "And what else did he offer?"

"Hospitality. I chatted away the night with his younger sister. We exchanged recipes." Not exactly true but close enough. "Sheriff Wolf was occupied with his investigation."

Attention was diverted from Saida when an ambulance arrived and turned down the driveway. The lack of siren meant only one thing: a death.

"Murder," said the guy with floppy hair. "Princess, do you know who was killed? Was it Granger?"

Truthfully, she answered, "I don't know."

In a news-seeking herd, the reporters moved away from her. The cameramen aimed their lenses toward the small house where several police vehicles were parked. Once again, the case had taken a deadly turn.

Saida found herself alone with the female reporter. She lowered her microphone and flashed a huge, red grin. "To tell the truth, I couldn't care less about the murder," she said. "I do entertainment news, and I'm here to see you."

"Have we met before?"

"I've been on a couple of red carpets where you were

strutting your stuff." Though it seemed impossible, her smile got even bigger. "Just between us girls, what do you think of Jake Wolf? Gorgeous, right? I wouldn't mind parking my stilettos under his bed. Right?"

"Between us," Saida mimicked the insincere phrase, "his appearance isn't important to me."

"Oh, please. He's turning into a celebrity himself. Tons of women are glued to the daily press briefing and fantasizing about long, cold Wyoming nights."

This woman was dying to turn her and Jake into a couple, which would have been much to Saida's liking. But definitely inappropriate. She didn't want to mess up Jake's career.

She lowered her gaze. "My only concern is my brother's safety. I'm so afraid for what might be happening to him."

The reporter scowled. "How come I don't know much about your brother?"

"He and the other COIN princes don't spend as much time in America as I do. A shame, really." Pushing this aggressive woman toward the others was purely evil, but Efraim had been a jerk and deserved to be tortured by the media. "They're all young and handsome…and unmarried."

The reporter murmured, "I should check them out."

Saida nodded as though dismissing her. "Please excuse me."

She went to where Nasim was standing. The big yellow Hummer separated them from the reporters and cameramen. Though they were close enough for her to hear them clamoring and demanding answers from the deputy who stood stalwartly blocking the road, she was no longer the object of their attention.

She looked up at her companion and bodyguard. "How did I do?"

"Nicely," he said.

"You didn't mention that someone was murdered."

"I was not told," he said. "Following the instructions of Sheriff Wolf, I entered the hovel of Mr. Granger with my weapon drawn. Mr. Granger was not in residence."

Though she wanted to see Jake and go over the photographs, she assumed he would be busy with the murder investigation for some time. Her suspicions and deductions would have to wait.

She hadn't thought that the process of investigating would require so much patience. Waiting was hard. Amir had been missing for weeks, and she wanted to take action.

As her gaze drifted along the line of the barbed-wire fence beside the shoulder of the road, she got an idea. Taking matters into her own hands shouldn't be a problem. As long as Nasim was along to protect her, she wouldn't get into trouble.

She reached for the door handle on the passenger side. "There's someone we need to talk with."

Chapter Twelve

When Burt Maddox said he was a neighbor of Chad Granger, he wasn't kidding. A quick check on her computer showed Maddox's address to be less than a mile from where they were parked.

Though Saida had no right to interrogate the former sheriff, she suspected that Maddox was either connected to the crimes or had information about them. In reviewing the photos Danny had taken, she'd spotted Maddox in the crowd more than once. He'd been hanging around, watching. And he'd found the truck. As Nasim had pointed out, there was too much coincidence.

If her bodyguard hadn't been accompanying her, she never would have gone to Maddox's house. But Nasim was right here, scowling with unspoken disapproval as he turned at the neatly lettered sign for Maddox Horse Ranch.

"You don't like this," she said. "You don't think I should get involved."

"As one who protects you, I prefer for you to be safe in your suite at the resort. However, I comprehend the need for interrogation. I think your partner should be Sheriff Wolf."

"I couldn't agree more."

In contrast to Granger's shabby, downtrodden ranch, this property was well-maintained. A white-washed fence enclosed a large field where two chestnut Arabian horses chased each other through the sunshine. At the far end of a paved circle drive, the sprawling white house featured a peaked roof and a wraparound porch with a screened section at one end. The house reminded her more of a genteel horse farm in Virginia than a rugged Wyoming ranch.

Maddox stepped down from the porch to greet them. "Princess Saida," he said. "I wondered how long it would take you royals to realize that you were close to the finest horse ranch in the West."

Seriously? He thought she'd come here to shop? It wouldn't hurt to play along. "Are you planning to expand your business to international markets?"

"Let's just say I've had interest from others."

"Who?"

"That's confidential."

She didn't exactly know what to make of Big Burt Maddox. With his doughy body and too-tight shirt, he looked like a clown, but not friendly. A mean clown.

He asked, "Do you ride, Princess?"

"Yes."

Behind her, Nasim snorted. As well as teaching her to shoot and drive, he'd been her equestrian instructor. When she introduced him, he offered Maddox a compliment. "Your Arab horses are spirited. Two-year-olds?"

"That's right," Maddox said. "Are you a man who knows horses?"

"I appreciate a fine thoroughbred. In the stables of Jamala, we have a matched set of gray Arabs, descended from horses that once belonged to King Farouk." Nasim looked over his shoulder toward the two magnificent horses in the field. "Will you be racing them?"

"If I could find the right trainer, I'd take my Arabians all the way to the Kentucky Derby."

Raising horses was expensive. Race horses, even more

so. Saida wondered how Maddox could afford this ranch. Supposedly, he'd made lucrative deals when he was sheriff. What else would he do to raise money?

She asked, "May we look at your stables?"

Though Maddox was grinning, his close-set eyes were anything but welcoming. He stared at her with an unblinking intensity, sizing her up and trying to decide if she was a potential customer. "Are you looking to buy?"

As a princess, her interest in purchasing was seldom questioned. Anyone who dealt with royalty assumed that she was capable of purchasing anything her heart desired. The fact that Maddox had asked indicated a crass nature.

She put on her very best regal manner. "Perhaps I will see a horse that pleases me."

Maddox hitched up his belt under his belly. "What do you think Jake Wolf would say if you bought a horse from me?"

"Sheriff Wolf's opinion is unimportant."

"Is that so?" He obviously didn't believe her. "Don't get me wrong, Princess, I'd be happy to sell you a pony or two, but you didn't come here looking to buy. I'd wager that you didn't even know I owned a horse ranch until you turned into my driveway."

He was more perceptive than she'd expected—not intelligent but shrewd. She made one last attempt to avoid hostility. "Won't you please show me around? If you refuse, I might think you have something to hide."

"Jake sent you here," he accused. "He knew I wouldn't talk to him, so he sent you."

"Sheriff Wolf doesn't know I'm here."

"Doesn't know much of anything," Maddox gloated. "At that press conference, I made him look like a damn fool. He's been running around chasing his tail while I located the truck."

Saida abandoned her flimsy pretense and confronted Maddox directly. "What made you suspect Granger?"

"For one thing, I know what he drives. That's the difference between me and Jake. He doesn't know his way around the county. Not like I do. I've lived here all my life. This is my land."

"One might argue that these lands belonged to the Native Americans long before your ancestors settled here."

"The Arapaho?" His upper lip curled in disgust. "Those Indians can't even manage their own reservation. They don't deserve to own land."

Apparently, politically correctness wasn't part of Maddox's vocabulary. "Is that why you opposed Jake for sheriff? Because he's Native American?"

"Sheriff is my job. Mine. I held that position for fifteen years. And I will be sheriff again."

She thought of how seriously Jake took his responsibilities and how hard he worked. It was difficult to imagine how Maddox found time to be sheriff and run his horse ranch. "You already have a thriving business."

"Damn right I do."

"How do you find qualified employees?" she asked.

"I've only got three full-time people, including the housekeeper I had to hire when my wife moved back to Cheyenne to take care of her parents. Good riddance to her. I'm glad she's gone."

As the anger built inside him, he seemed to expand. His complexion turned mottled and ruddy. If Saida was going to get any useful information, she had to ask her questions quickly before he exploded. "Do you hire part-time help?"

"Why do you want to know?"

"Did Chad Granger work for you?"

"I'm done talking." He pointed toward the gate. "Get out. You foreigners are all alike. Think you're better than us. Well,

I got news for you, Princess. Real Americans—red-white-and-blue Americans like me—don't like your kind. Get off my land."

Red-white-and-blue idiots! She straightened her spine and retreated with her dignity intact. She hadn't lost her cool, but Big Burt Maddox appeared to be on the verge of an epic eruption. He was an angry man, filled with hate. And, therefore, dangerous.

JAKE SHOULD HAVE BEEN angry when he heard about Saida's visit to Maddox. But every single one of the COIN royals had meddled in his investigation. There was no stopping them, no point being outraged, especially since he liked Saida a whole lot better than any of the others. He wasn't mad at her. Just concerned.

She needed his help, more than she knew. In his pocket, he carried the evidence he'd taken from the murder scene. Saida's earring. He couldn't stop thinking about her stolen Beretta.

He'd left his office around six, gone home for dinner and was grateful to find that Maggie had prepared a simple recipe—pork chops, veggies and corn bread. He helped himself and carried his plate to the dining room table.

His sister plunked herself down in the seat to his right. "What's going on?"

He had the murder investigation orchestrated. The forensic people were analyzing fingerprints and trace evidence. The coroner had the body. Deputy Wheeler was doing follow-up interviews with potential witnesses, while the other deputies and local police searched for the missing sedan and for Chad Granger. The FBI Special Agent assigned to the case was pursuing an investigation into the background of the victim and his connections to Granger.

None of this was information that Maggie needed to know. Jake shrugged. "The usual."

"Tell me about the dead man."

"Not much to tell." William Dormund was a man on the skids. A disbarred lawyer who had set himself up as a private investigator, he operated out of his duplex with a couple of file cabinets and a cell phone. "He's from Cheyenne and used to be an attorney."

"That's not what I meant, Jake." She punched his arm to get his full attention. "I want to know about your feelings."

"I'm dealing with it, Maggie. One of the reasons I came home early was to make peace within myself."

"If there's anything I can do—"

"I'll let you know."

Neither of them practiced many of the Arapaho traditions, but they both believed that life was sacred. *We are all connected, all born from the earth. A hunter offers thanks to his prey for providing meat. A farmer blesses the bounty of his fields before harvest.*

Earlier today, Jake had stared into the sightless eyes of a murder victim. It was important for him to acknowledge that death, to pay attention to the passing of this man's spirit.

Some years ago, when he was a cop in Cheyenne, Jake and his partner had been in pursuit of an armed suspect. They'd been fired upon. There had been no choice but to engage. Jake had shot the suspect in the chest and had held him while he breathed his last breath and the light inside him had been extinguished.

Taking a life had changed him. He would never become jaded. Death must always be treated with respect.

But he wasn't about to talk about his feelings with his baby sister, even if she was a psychology major. He changed the topic. "Since the victim was in the legal community in

Cheyenne, I contacted Oscar Pollack. He promised to ask around for me."

Maggie brightened. "How's Oscar?"

"Keeping busy at work, and his family is happy. Hard to believe that his twins are already in kindergarten."

"I should zip down to Cheyenne and pay him a visit before I go back to school."

Jake wouldn't mind having Maggie out of the way until this investigation was over. "No problem. I can hire one of the teenagers next door to exercise the horses."

"But I'd miss out on all this excitement."

"Which reminds me," he said, "Saida and Nasim are on their way over here. She wants us to go through the photos that—"

"Saida is coming here?" Maggie stared down at her oversize T-shirt and baggy plaid boxers. "I've got to change clothes."

She bolted from the table and raced upstairs. Being raised with sisters, Jake wasn't surprised by her reaction. Though women asked for an opinion from their husband or mate, they usually dressed to impress other women. The only exception might be lingerie. Filmy gowns. Shimmering satin. Glowing silk.

His mind drifted to Saida. Maggie considered the princess to be a fashion icon, but he was more interested in what Saida would wear to bed. He imagined a see-through black robe over a lace bra and skimpy panties. Or something in a beige tone, like that naked shirt she'd worn the other day. Or nothing at all. She might be a woman who slept in the nude.

The fantasy occupied his mind and almost erased the ugly residue of the day. When he looked down, he realized that he'd finished every bite of his dinner.

He carried his plate to the kitchen and returned in time to answer the doorbell for Saida and Nasim.

The princess wasted no time with apologies. "I talked to Maddox, and he definitely has something to hide. I think Chad Granger worked for him part-time."

"You're right."

Her caramel eyes opened wide. "Do you know for sure?"

"I sent Wheeler over to interview Maddox and the men who work at his ranch. Granger filled in part-time on a regular basis. But not for the past couple of weeks. They also confirmed that Granger recently came into money."

"Speaking of money," she said, "that beautiful horse ranch must cost a fortune to maintain. If Maddox needs cash, he might be willing to take a payoff."

"He's willing."

"Do you have proof?"

"I wish I did. When Maddox was sheriff, he had his greedy fingers in a lot of lucrative deals. There were payoffs and bribes. And a lack of concrete evidence. He knows how to cover his tracks."

Maggie bounded down the stairs in a fresh outfit that was purple and gray. As she approached Saida, she paused for half a second before enveloping the princess in a hug. After gushing over Saida's jacket that looked like a pinstriped windbreaker to Jake, Maggie grabbed Nasim's hand and pumped.

"Anybody hungry?" she asked.

"I appreciate your gracious offer," Nasim said. "A most savory aroma emanates from your kitchen."

"Follow me."

Maggie drew the impeccably dressed bodyguard behind her like a pull toy on a string, leaving Jake and Saida together in the entryway. They were semialone. If he whispered her name, only she would hear him. If he reached toward her, he could glide his fingers through her silky black hair. He could kiss her. No one else would see.

Not that he intended to do any of those things.

She set her laptop on the dining room table. "I want to go through these photos that I got from Danny. There are several faces that appear repeatedly. Maddox is one of them."

Her photographic evidence merited consideration, but there was another concern at the front of his mind. "Before we get started, there's something I need to tell you."

She looked up expectantly. "I'm guessing this isn't good news."

"Good guess."

He reached into his pocket, took out the dime-size earring and held it between his fingers so she could see. "This is yours. I recognized the design."

"I didn't even know it was missing. Did it fall out of my luggage?"

He took her wrist, lifted her hand and placed the earring in the center of her palm. "I found it beside the murder victim."

Her fingers clenched, but she didn't pull away from him. He felt the tension in her wrist. Those fine bones were so delicate, so fragile.

Her gaze searched his face. "I don't understand."

Jake didn't have a clear explanation. The murderer was sending a message. "Could be meant as a threat."

"I'm already aware of the danger," she said. "The truck that ran me off the road was kind of obvious."

"It could be meant to throw suspicion on you. A piece of your jewelry is found near the victim. You're implicated."

"Am I a suspect?"

"Not in my book. At the time of death, you were with me. That's a pretty solid alibi."

"But you don't control what other people think," she said. "Maddox made it pretty clear that real Americans don't like foreigners."

"Maddox is an idiot."

"There's a simple explanation for why my earring was

there. When the killer went through my luggage, he stole my earring." She inhaled a sharp gasp. "And my Beretta. Oh, my God, Jake. Was my gun used to kill that man?"

The murder weapon hadn't yet been found.

Chapter Thirteen

Saida didn't want to believe that her gun had been used in the murder. A man's life had ended because she brought that gun to Wyoming. The tension she'd held inside became a tremor, and she pulled her wrist from Jake's grasp, not wanting him to notice her weakness.

"His name was William," she remembered.

"William Dormund."

She struggled to stay calm, but her pulse was racing. "This isn't my fault. I didn't pull the trigger. There's no reason for me to feel guilty."

"There's a reason to feel," he said.

"To feel what?"

"A man died. Respect should be paid."

Death wasn't something she liked to think about. She was only twenty-two and a princess. Her life was supposed to be a fairy tale filled with dances, parties and expensive things. But death wasn't a stranger. Both her parents had passed away, and she'd lost other relatives and friends. She knew what it meant to grieve. But why should she be devastated by the murder of a man she'd never met?

This wasn't the way she wanted the investigation to turn out. They should be moving forward, uncovering information that would lead to her brother.

When Maggie and Nasim came back into the dining room from the kitchen, Saida turned her head away so her body-guard wouldn't see that she was upset.

Jake spoke for her. "We're going outside for a minute."

"Something wrong?" Maggie asked.

Too many somethings to explain. Being implicated in a murder was just another knot in this tangled mess. Saida forced a smile. "We'll be right back."

Outside, she rested one hand on the railing. In the other, she held the black earring with the crossed sword design. "I just want to throw this thing and never see it again. But I don't suppose that's permitted. This is evidence."

"Not exactly." Jake stepped up beside her. "I found the earring. And I told no one."

Surprised, she looked up at him. "You broke the chain of evidence?"

"Sometimes you have to do what's right instead of what's legal."

She never would have thought that super-responsible Jake would venture outside the boundaries of police procedure. He'd violated the rules to protect her. Maybe he cared about her. She hoped it was so.

"How do you deal with it?" she asked. "The violence?"

He shrugged.

"I really want to know." She hated this dark feeling of regret and undeserved guilt. "Police work shows you the very worst in people. You see the hatred and cruelty that leads to murder. How do you keep that from making you crazy?"

"I can show you."

Was he talking about some kind of release exercise, like running or yelling at the top of his lungs or twirling like a dervish? Or maybe he wanted to show her something more personal. Maybe he was coming on to her, and that would be lovely. Their first kiss made her yearn for more. "I'm ready."

WITHIN TWENTY MINUTES, Saida was astride one of Jake's horses—a gray mare named Rainy. Though it had been a couple of years since she'd been riding and she wasn't really dressed for this type of exercise in her low-heeled brogues and designer jacket, she felt right at home in the saddle. Some things you never forget.

The problem was where to put her gun. If she stuffed her purse into a saddle bag, she wouldn't be able to reach her weapon quickly enough to respond to a threat. She lengthened the strap on her purse and wore it across her chest. Not a fashionable solution but a practical one.

Her own appearance was secondary to watching Jake. He embodied every Western movie hero she'd ever seen. His flat-brimmed cowboy hat was pulled low on his forehead. His dusty boots stuck in the stirrups. He'd changed from his uniform into a denim shirt with the sleeves rolled up. He wore his handgun at his hip and carried a hunting rifle behind the saddle.

Jake was the opposite of the metrosexual men she usually dated. He was a real man, a manly man. Her friends in Beverly Hills would never believe someone like him existed. Subtly, she snuck her cell phone from her purse and took a couple photos. Did this make her a paparazzo?

Their only supplies were a couple of bottles of water which meant they wouldn't be going far, but Jake hadn't told her their destination. Anticipation buzzed through her; this was an adventure.

As they rode from the barn, Nasim and Maggie stood at the fence watching. An odd twosome, they had very little in common, but they fit together like salt and pepper. Nasim had immediately agreed when Jake said they were going for a ride, and Saida suspected that both he and Maggie were doing a bit of matchmaking.

She followed as Jake rode toward the fence. Maggie

opened the gate. Smiling up at her brother, she spoke a few syllables that Saida didn't understand.

"This way." Jake motioned to her. "We have to stick to the road for half a mile to get to open land. Single file."

She fell into line behind his big roan horse that was named Jimmy in honor of Jim Thorpe, the famous Native-American athlete who Jake claimed as one of his idols. Riding at the edge of the road seemed dangerous to her. They'd be vulnerable to an attack from a car. But Jake knew everyone; he exchanged waves with all the vehicles that went past them.

Nonetheless, she was relieved when they reached open land. Their horses ambled through a grassy field dotted with daisies and bright red wildflowers. In the distance, she saw the peaks of the Wind River Range. After living in California for so many years, she wasn't accustomed to such a transparent, cloudless sky. The dry air brushed lightly against her skin.

She rode up beside Jake and asked, "What did Maggie say as we were leaving?"

"An Arapaho blessing. She was wishing me good fortune."

"To do what? Where are we going?"

"Be patient."

In Wind River County, life moved at a different pace than she was accustomed to. Though she was all in favor of experiencing peace and nature and regularly attended yoga classes, she was itching for action.

Jake seemed to be leading her toward a forested area where she assumed they'd be going single file again. If she wanted to talk to him, she ought to do it now.

"I'm looking at the big picture in the investigation," she said. "And I'm trying to make sense of it. First, somebody tries to kidnap me. Now, I'm being framed for murder. Why?"

"I'd guess that whoever is behind these threats—the money man who paid off Granger—is motivated by something that's happening in your little country on the other side of the world."

"I've told you before. I have no power in Jamala."

"Maybe you can't make laws or start wars or dictate policy, but don't underestimate yourself, Saida. I've seen you in action. You have influence."

"Amir listens to me," she admitted.

"And Amir is the key," he said. "The threat to you is actually directed at him. When you showed up, Granger and Dormund tried to grab you. Why? Because you had something they wanted. I'm guessing they thought you knew how to contact your brother."

She nodded. "Which is good news because it means Amir isn't in the clutches of the bad guys."

"We'll assume he's in hiding. What would it take to draw him into the open?"

"If I was kidnapped."

"That was likely their first plan, but you were too fast for them."

And Jake had appeared to rescue her. She glanced over at the man in the saddle. A reluctant hero, he wasn't the kind of man who needed medals or recognition. She doubted that he even realized how incredible he was.

"What else?" he asked. "What else would make your brother respond?"

She thought for a moment. "If I was suspected of murder and thrown in jail, Amir would come forth to protect me."

"When Granger went digging through your luggage and lucked out by finding a gun, he grabbed it. And your jewelry." He paused, frowned. "I don't think Granger is smart enough to figure out that he could frame you. Somebody else came up with that plan."

"Lucky for me, I have an airtight alibi."

"Being implicated in murder is still bad news," he said. "It discredits you. Makes you a suspect instead of a victim."

"Why should I care what people think of me?"

"You're not naive," he said. "When it comes to ruling a country, politics are always involved."

She knew he was right. Public opinion was important, even in a sheikdom. "Your problems with Maddox are a mirror image of mine. He's out to destroy you."

He turned toward her. "Are you ready to give these ponies some real exercise?"

"Right behind you."

He flicked his reins and tapped the flanks of his horse with his heels. The big roan took off, galloping across the field. The sheer beauty of man and horse stunned her. She was tempted to whip out her cell phone camera again, but there was no way she could capture the power of the moment in a single shot. This would have to be a memory, something she knew she'd never forget.

She gave her horse the cue to run. With a toss of her head, Rainy charged forward.

Saida's riding lessons had been geared toward formal dressage maneuvers, but she loved to race. Her thighs tensed, holding on tightly. She adjusted her balance to Rainy's gait as they rushed forward, running parallel to the line of the trees. Wind whipped through her hair and grazed her cheeks. Her pulse accelerated. Her blood was pumping. She felt alive, exhilarated.

Riding fast jostled the dark thoughts from her mind. She forgot to be confused and disturbed. The sheer physical excitement of the moment overwhelmed everything else.

At the edge of the forest, she reined her horse. She could feel the smile stretching her lips, and Jake's grin matched hers. His white teeth made a brilliant contrast against his dark skin.

"I get it," she said. "This is how you deal with stress."

"It's momentary relief." His horse pawed the ground, ready for more action. "Physical activity is a quick fix."

"Like sex. I always feel better after…" She pinched her lips together. She hadn't meant to be so personal. "That wasn't appropriate."

"Don't worry. I didn't think you were a virgin princess."

"A word of advice. Never say that to Nasim."

He wheeled around and directed Jimmy along a path that led into the thick pine forest. As Rainy followed, Saida's spirits were still high. The Wyoming experience was unlike anything she'd ever done. She'd sailed on hundred-foot yachts, gone diving at the Great Barrier reef, bungee jumped and skied on a glacier. She'd seen the view from the top of the Eiffel Tower, visited the secret catacombs in Egypt and watched her brother run with the bulls in Pamplona.

Riding with Jake was different. It was better, definitely better. When she was with him, there was an excitement that touched her more deeply than an exotic trek.

For a while, they followed a narrow creek with water as shimmering as diamonds. Tall thickets of berries and lilac branches brushed against her legs as Rainy picked her way along the path. The air was scented with pine. After a bit of an uphill ride, they emerged from the forest onto a rocky ledge overlooking a wide canyon.

The vista was enormous and spectacular. Sunset colored the skies with a rosy glow and reflected rich golden hues on the wispy clouds.

"We're here," Jake said as he dismounted.

She climbed down from her horse and stood beside him, staring at that awesome sky. Their hands were almost touching.

She whispered, "Is this where you come to find relief?"

"Being outside in nature has a way of healing any wounds," he said. "But this isn't what I wanted to show you."

"I'm glad you brought me here."

"You were troubled. The murder got to you."

"I could have handled it," she said quickly. "I'm not the kind of person who falls apart."

"It got to me, too." His voice was as low as the rustle of wind through the pine boughs. "The rage and hatred that drives a man to murder is a poison, and nobody is immune. Today, I stood over the body of a dead man. I have to deal with that."

As he walked toward the rocks at the edge of the trees, he continued, "I don't consider myself a religious man, and I don't follow the ways of my tribe. But I believe we are all part of creation. Everything that lives is sacred."

A huge slab of rounded granite formed an overhang that protected a fire ring with charred branches and ashes in the middle. He asked, "Have you ever heard of a sweat lodge?"

"Sure. I've lived in Southern California for a long time."

"What does that mean?"

"There's a guru or medium or a shaman on every street corner. Some of them actually make sense and help people. Most are loons." She knew a lot of people who had spiritual advisors. "Anyway, I've heard that sweat lodges are like a sauna where everybody gets naked and has visions."

"That sounds like a hell of a lot more fun than my version." He grinned. "Especially the naked part."

She liked that idea, too. Getting naked with him and working up a sweat would be perfect. With a wicked smile, she asked, "Is that what you wanted me to see?"

Ignoring her double entendre, he went behind the fire circle and hunkered down. With a burnt stick, he poked at the ashes. "Most tribes have their own version of a sweat lodge. Typically, it's a tentlike structure, a wickiup, with a low-burning fire in the middle. You sit there and sweat."

"Like a sauna," she said.

"Not naked, though."

"Too bad."

"You open your mind and your heart, sending your spirit on a vision quest that teaches you important lessons about yourself and your place in the world."

Standing on the opposite side of the fire circle, she pointed out the obvious. "There's no wickiup here."

"And this isn't really a sweat lodge," he said. "I don't have time to meditate for hours, but this works for me."

She was ready to try anything. At the moment, she wasn't feeling too bummed, but her dark thoughts hadn't disappeared. They lurked in the back of her mind. "How do we do it? Are we supposed to chant?"

"I usually take off the things that keep me tied to my everyday life. And I usually build a small fire. But not today." He left the fire circle and came toward her. "There isn't time to make sure a fire is completely out. And I'm not taking off my gun."

"Separating from everyday life. Got it."

Standing beside her in an open space between the trees and the edge of the rocks, he took off his hat and dropped it onto the ground. Then he removed his wristwatch.

She followed his example by peeling off her jacket. Her scarf, her rings and her bracelets were added to the pile. She unfastened her necklace and her earrings. These were simple actions but somehow symbolic. She was shedding possessions, distancing herself from her very complicated life.

"Do you ever meditate?" he asked.

"I've tried." But there was usually too much going on inside her head to reach a state of complete openness.

"Close your eyes." He took her shoulders and turned her.

"You're facing north. A direction of strength and power. Breathe slowly. Feel a white light pouring through you."

Standing with her eyes closed made her a bit disoriented, so she sat on the rock. Her pulse calmed. The clean air soothed her. The setting sun warmed her shoulders.

The duties and privileges of being a princess were gone. In this moment, she was only a woman.

Chapter Fourteen

Jake had walked this path many times before, but he had always been alone. Having Saida with him in his meditation felt different but right. He knew she'd been troubled when she thought her gun might have ended a man's life, and her concern for a life—any life—was similar to his own understanding.

They had much in common. Though born a world apart and raised in completely different circumstances, they shared a deep understanding. Jake wished that he'd had a guide when he first confronted violence. He might be able to help her find peace.

He unbuttoned his shirt and cast it onto the pile of their earthly belongings. His holster weighed heavy on his hip, but he needed to be armed, even though he didn't expect for anyone to find them.

This particular spot was special to him. Even before he bought his house, he'd come to this ledge overlooking the canyon. Though he didn't really believe in a sacred space, this came close.

Facing north, he stood behind her seated form and raised his arms to welcome the strength he needed. His spirit opened. His feet sent down roots deep into the earth where he drew nourishment.

After a moment, he leaned down and gently rested his

hands on her shoulders. The connection between them was palpable. "Do you feel it?"

"Yes." Her voice was as sweet as a wood flute. "Warm."

"Keep your eyes closed and turn in a half circle."

Instead of standing, she scooted around to switch positions. "Is this right?"

"There isn't right or wrong. It's whatever feels good." But he made sure that she was facing south. "This is the direction of growth."

Though he was looking toward trees and rocks, the sunset spilled yellow across the land. Their horses were tethered in the trees, and he imagined the healthy glow of their life force. He loved the south—the sense of unbounded creation wherein all things were possible.

"I hear something," she said. "The echo of my heartbeat."

Her blood was pumping, healing her, helping her to grow.

He directed her toward the east, the direction of red sunrise that brought enlightenment. He peered through the trunks of pine trees and looked up to the sky. "This way is wisdom. Here is where I remember, and I think."

In his mind's eye, he replayed the moment when he had looked down on the murdered man. Jake imagined the course of the bullet, heard the last breath, felt the loss and the darkness that accompanied sudden death.

Could he have prevented the murder? As sheriff of Wind River County, it was his duty to keep the peace. Had he done as much as he could? There was always more; no one was perfect. He would continue to try, to seek the truth. He needed to be smart and to bring an end to the violence that had started when Amir disappeared.

He didn't know what Saida was thinking. Her meditation would be particular to her. She exhaled a sigh, and her shoulders slumped.

Crouching beside her, he asked, "What is it?"

"I understand." Another sigh. "I can't make things different."

He took her hand and helped her to stand. Turning her to the west where the sunset painted the sky, he stood behind her. "Open your eyes."

She gasped. "So beautiful."

"When the sun goes down, the west becomes dark. This is the way of the spirit. I'm thinking of the one who died."

He grieved for the murdered man and hoped his essence would find peace. In his mind, Jake sent the spirit on its way. "Goodbye, William."

Saida leaned her back against his chest. He encircled her with his arms and held her. They stood and watched as the sun dipped behind the peaks.

When she turned toward him, her eyes were bright. Her spirit was strong and wise. He lowered his head and kissed her soft, inviting lips. The inside of her mouth was hot.

Meditation had refreshed all his senses and given him clarity. He heard her breath and the surging of her heart. He smelled the scent of jasmine. The smooth skin of her arm glided across his bare back as she molded herself against him.

He wanted to touch every part of her. His fingers slipped through her silken hair. His hand slid down her back and explored her slender waist and the fullness of her hips. Though she had the slender body of a fashion model, her curves were womanly. He slid his hand under her shirt and found her breast. Her tight nipple poked against the lace of her bra, and she trembled when his fingers tweaked the delicate tip.

She leaned back in his arms and looked up at him. She was so lovely. Her hair, her skin, the arch of her neck, everything. This moment was as close to perfection as he'd ever been.

"I don't want this to end," she said.

"Neither do I."

He wanted to carry her into the forest, spread his shirt on the ground and make love to her. He wanted to spend the whole night holding her in his arms and counting the stars as they appeared one by one in a velvet sky.

That wasn't going to happen.

When they set out from his house, he hadn't planned on making love to her. He hadn't been prepared. No condom. No way was this ever going to happen to him again.

"We should head back," he said.

"I'd rather not."

She nestled her head against his chest. Her embrace tightened. Resisting her was killing him. From this day forward, he'd always carry one or two…or seven condoms.

He kissed the top of her head and inhaled the jasmine fragrance of her shampoo. "We have plenty of time."

"That's right, isn't it?" Reluctantly, she separated from him. "Even after we find Amir, there's no reason I can't stay in Wyoming for the whole summer."

"Sure," he said. "Six suitcases. That's enough clothes to last for months."

"Speaking of which…" She crossed the rocks to the place where they'd piled their belongings and pivoted to face him. "Much as I hate to go back, we should get dressed. Even though I much prefer you shirtless."

"Given an opportunity to judge," he said, "I'm pretty sure I'd say the same."

She knelt to pick through the tiny bits of gold and silver she'd discarded. "I kind of hate to put on all my jewelry. Getting rid of this stuff made me feel free."

"And how do you feel now?"

Her lips pursed as she paused to think.

He really liked the way she considered before speaking. Sometimes she rebounded in an instant. But she often resisted the urge to blurt out the first words that came to mind.

"Strong," she said. "And calm."

He would add one more word: *loving*.

AS DUSK SETTLED, JAKE rode slowly back to his house, side by side with the princess. Their horses ambled in a comfortable gait, not in a rush. And their conversation was equally easygoing. By unspoken agreement, they didn't discuss the investigation.

"This might be my favorite time of day," he said. "When all the chores are done, and you can settle back and reflect."

"That's not my experience," she said. "Early evening is when my day starts. I usually have to be somewhere. Some kind of event or appearance."

"You're a night owl."

"Mostly. I love sleeping late in the morning. Waking up slowly, stretching and yawning like a lazy cat. Then I have my espresso. Do you like your coffee strong?"

"Strong and black," he said. "None of that whipped cream and sprinkle stuff."

"What about Vietnamese coffee?"

"Never tried it."

"It's an absolute treat. Made with sweetened condensed milk. I could make it for you. The best breakfast in the world with a croissant and butter."

Discussing breakfast probably wasn't the smartest thing to do. Though he wanted to make love to her, he knew it wasn't appropriate.

As they approached his house, he spotted Nasim and Maggie in the driveway shooting hoops. Saida's tall, formal bodyguard had removed his jacket and necktie but still wore his shoulder holster.

Maggie waved as they drew closer. "We've been having a great time. Nasim showed me some karate moves."

"Krav Maga," Nasim said. "It is a hand-to-hand combat

technique developed in Israel. Efficient and potentially lethal."

Jake dismounted at the edge of the driveway. "Nothing good can come from my baby sister knowing lethal combat techniques."

"What if I'm attacked?" She braced herself. "Come on, Wolfman, make a move."

"Nasim taught me the same moves," Saida whispered to him. "I'd advise against trying to attack Maggie. You could be walking sideways for a week."

"You win, sis." Jake raised both hands in surrender. "Would you mind taking care of the horses while the princess and I go through these photos?"

"Chicken," she taunted. "You're a big, old, fat chicken."

"You know what Mama always says."

Maggie dropped her fighting stance. "Better a wise chicken than a dead duck."

"Come, Maggie." Nasim picked up the reins. "I will help with the horses."

Without an argument, she joined him and they headed toward the barn. Never at a loss for something to say, Maggie chattered happily while Nasim nodded and occasionally gave a snort.

Jake shot a glance toward Saida. "Should we be worried that they're getting along so well?"

"Nasim is a natural teacher. When I was growing up, he enjoyed our lessons as much as I did. I keep telling him that he should open a school in Jamala, but he's not interested in business."

"Does he have kids?"

"Four sons, five daughters. Twelve grandchildren." Saida gave him a smile. "Even with a brood like that, he keeps pushing me to get married and to reproduce."

Just like Maggie. Now, Jake was certain that the two of

them were arranging time for him and Saida to be alone with each other. As if such a marriage would work? Sure, there was a heavy-duty attraction between them. But he wasn't planning to leave Wyoming, not after he'd finally gotten himself elected as sheriff. And he couldn't imagine the princess living here.

In the dining room, they focused on the investigation. Saida had printed out selected photos that Danny had taken and she spread ten of them across the tabletop.

"These are the best group shots," she said. "I've noticed several people who appear multiple times. The most obvious is Big Burt Maddox."

"Not a surprise." Of course, Maddox would be snooping around, watching for ways that Jake would fail as sheriff.

She pointed to another face in the crowd. "This man shows up four times."

"Chad Granger. I noticed him the first time I looked at Danny's pictures. If I'd acted then, questioned him, I might have been able to arrest him before he ran."

He pointed to a long-faced cowboy. "This guy works for Maddox. Can't remember his name."

"Here's an anomaly." She indicated a small, gray-haired woman with bright eyes. "This lady shows up on three different occasions."

"She has a quilt store." Jake didn't really think this elderly woman was a criminal mastermind. "She's probably just a fan of royalty, but it wouldn't hurt to pay her a visit tomorrow."

"May I come with you?"

"You bet. If she likes royals, she'll be thrilled to meet a famous princess."

"There's no need to be snarky." She drew herself up and put on her regal expression. "Many people are fascinated by royal families."

"I get it," he said. "Ceremony is important. It provides continuity."

She pointed out many others. Some were reporters or paparazzi; it made sense for them to be on the scene. Others were part of the royal entourage. A couple of them were security people or employees at the Wind River Ranch and Resort.

Saida pointed out a man who stayed far to the edge of the crowd as though trying not to be noticed. In another photo, he had turned slightly away. "Do you know him?"

Jake studied the photograph of a broad-shouldered man with thick, dark hair and deep-set eyes. "There's something real familiar about him. I think he owns a ranch outside town."

"His name?"

"I'm not sure." While campaigning, Jake had met many of the locals. "I can ask Wheeler. He's lived here all his life."

"He looks like he's trying to avoid the camera."

Jake had made a mistake by not going after Granger right away. He didn't intend to falter again. "We need to find this man. Right away."

Maggie and Nasim returned to the house. She bounded up to the table. "These are the photos from that paparazzo guy, right?"

Jake pointed to the mystery man. "Do you recognize him?"

"I think so." She leaned down and squinted. "Earlier this summer, I filled in at the café in Dumont for one of the waitresses who was having a baby. I met just about everybody."

"Well?" he asked.

"He's a rancher. Freeman. His last name is Freeman." She looked up at her brother. "You had a phone call while you were gone. I guess your cell wasn't getting reception."

"Did they leave a message?"

"He wanted you to call back as soon as possible. His name is A.J. or A.G., something like that."

"The A.G.," he said. "Attorney General. The Attorney General for the state of Wyoming?"

"Oh, wow." Maggie frowned. "He didn't say he was anybody important."

But he was. Jake doubted the Attorney General was calling with good news.

Chapter Fifteen

While Jake went upstairs to his bedroom to make his phone call, Saida decided it was a good time to check the messages on her own cell. In the living room, she sank into a comfortable-looking chair near the fireplace. As soon as her butt hit the cushions, she realized she was a bit sore. Her usual exercise regimen didn't include horseback riding or sitting on hard granite ledges. She adjusted her position, not wanting to be accused of acting like the princess who was so delicate she couldn't sleep if there was a pea under ten mattresses.

Her message box was full. Friends from California had tried to reach her, and she was tempted to call some of her girlfriends back and tell them about Jake. But how could she explain? Most of the women she knew wouldn't understand if she told them that she'd rode into the Wyoming sunset and meditated on the edge of a cliff with a bare-chested Arapaho sheriff.

They might be jealous. Saida smiled to herself. If she emailed one of the photos she'd taken of Jake, her friends would be gasping with envy. But she didn't want to share that moment.

The time she'd spent with Jake was deeply intimate, even more private than making love. When she'd taken off her jewelry and her designer jacket, she'd shed the identity she presented to the world. Completely vulnerable, she'd exposed her fears and her innermost hopes. And he'd held her, kept her safe. She couldn't entirely explain how she felt, much less chat about it with friends.

Scrolling down the list, she skipped to a message from Callie McGuire and returned that call. Since Callie might be contacting her in an official capacity as Assistant to the Secretary of Foreign Affairs, Saida used a formal tone. "This is Princess Saida Khalid."

"Thanks for returning my call," Callie said. "I have a big favor to ask."

A favor? That explained why Callie was calling instead of Efraim. He refused to acknowledge that Saida could be useful in any way, and he certainly wouldn't request her help. "How can I help, Callie?"

"The Cattlemen's Ball is tomorrow in Cheyenne. Someone from the COIN nations should make an appearance."

"Why?"

"A lot of important oil people will be there, people your brother has contacted."

"I know very little about my brother's business. Efraim or one of the other princes should handle this."

"It's not a business meeting," she said. "This is a matter of creating goodwill and assuring future partners that COIN is a viable partner."

Goodwill was Saida's forte. She knew how to be charming and create a positive impression, but she didn't want to abandon the investigation. "I came here to find my brother. Not to attend a ball."

Callie paused for a moment. "Efraim thinks it's important for you to smooth over any concerns investors might have."

"What kind of concerns?"

"Your brother's disappearance has created problems. There's a power struggle in Jamala."

Saida fired a glance at Nasim who stood in the doorway between the dining room and the kitchen, keeping an eye on her and Maggie at the same time. If Jamala was in turmoil, he should have told her. To Callie, she said, "I'll think about your request and call you back."

Saida bolted from the chair, too irritated to pay attention to the twinges from sore muscles. The heels of her brogues thumped on the hardwood floor as she charged toward Nasim. "Why didn't you tell me what was happening in Jamala?"

His nostrils flared. "The situation does not rise to a level of importance."

"Callie McGuire seems to think it's important." Saida would never raise her voice to Nasim; she respected him too much. "I expect Efraim to treat me like a brainless child, but I thought you would trust me."

"I have confidence in you, Saida."

"Tell me. Is there a power struggle?"

"Your brother has enemies in Jamala."

She didn't ask for names or affiliations; she was too distant from the situation. In the years since her father died and Amir took over the business of ruling their country, she'd only been home for a few vacations—times that had been filled with parties instead of attending council meetings.

"There isn't much I can do," she said, "but you should be in Jamala, watching over our interests."

"My duty is to protect you."

Saida glanced toward Maggie who was watching this exchange with wide, curious eyes. For a moment, Saida considered switching to Greek or Arabic, languages that both she and Nasim spoke fluently. But Saida didn't need to keep secrets from Jake's sister.

"Callie wants me to attend a ball in Cheyenne," she said. "To make it look to investors that everything is just fine in Jamala. Do you agree?"

"Amir has worked hard to develop the oil business. He would want you to attend this event." Nasim took out his cell phone. "I will make arrangements."

She stayed his hand before he could start punching in numbers. "There's only one way I'll agree to this. You must return to Jamala and put things in order. I don't know the political ins and outs, but you do."

"What of your safety?"

She arched an eyebrow. "You didn't seem so worried about me when I went riding off with Jake this afternoon."

"I trust Sheriff Jake Wolf," he said staunchly. "However, you are my responsibility."

"You're needed in Jamala." She lifted her chin. "Don't make me issue a royal command."

He gave a snort. Then he placed his right hand over his heart and bowed his head. "Yes, my princess."

Jake came down the staircase and strode into the kitchen. "What's going on here?"

Maggie gave him the rundown, starting with trouble in Jamala and ending with Saida attending the Cattlemen's Ball.

"As it turns out," Jake said, "I'll be going to Cheyenne, too. The state attorney general requested my presence. There's been a lot of bad publicity associated with what's been going on here, and I need to smooth some feathers."

"Excellent," Nasim said. "Sheriff Wolf will·accompany Princess Saida on a private jet. You will depart tomorrow at four o'clock. I shall make hotel reservations."

She watched Jake for his reaction. He might not want to be her bodyguard. The first time they had this conversation, he'd said he was too busy and preoccupied.

He smiled at her. "Excellent."

JAKE WOULD BE LEAVING town tomorrow. On a private jet? To attend a fancy-dress ball? Escorting a princess? He pushed all that stuff out of his head. Tomorrow, he'd worry about it.

Tonight, there was still work to do and not a minute to waste. With Saida in the passenger seat, he drove his SUV out of the driveway. His were the only headlights on the road. If Jake had been a big city cop, he'd have hit the accelerator and turned on the siren. He would have called for backup and dragged in ten patrol vehicles to make his point.

But this was Wind River County, where hardworking folks went to bed early, and ten o'clock was considered late to show up for a visit.

"Maggie was right," Jake said. "She identified the guy in the photos as Freeman. While I was on the phone, I looked him up on the internet. Wade Freeman owns a good-size cattle ranch and a website with his photo."

"A cattle rancher," she said. "Do you think he'll go to the event in Cheyenne?"

"Probably not. The Cattlemen's Ball isn't a stock show or a place to sell beef. Most ranchers couldn't care less about a dress-up party. If they're going to take time off, they'll go to the rodeo during Frontier Days in July."

"Who will be at the ball?"

"Some folks in the cattle industry, big money people and politicians like the attorney general."

"Callie said there would be oil investors."

"And their wives," he said. "Some ladies are always looking for a chance to show off and get prettied up."

"Like the wife of Burt Maddox?"

He glanced toward her. "What made you think of that?"

"When I went to see Maddox, he said that his wife had moved to Cheyenne to take care of her parents. Do you think she'll be at the event?"

"Oh, yeah. Mrs. Virginia Maddox loved being somebody important, the wife of the sheriff."

"I had the impression that she and Big Burt might not

be on the best of terms. He used the phrase 'good riddance' when referring to her."

"We'll want to talk to her."

The other thing he wanted to do in Cheyenne was to investigate William Dormund's background. The second phone call he'd returned when he went upstairs was to the FBI agent who had been investigating all the crimes associated with the COIN princes.

Earlier today, the agent had contacted the FBI branch operating out of Cheyenne. They'd done the standard investigative procedures: taking possession of Dormund's files, talking to friends and associates, reviewing the records for his phone calls and pulling his bank receipts. So far, they'd turned up a whole lot of nothing.

Dormund had worked on the fringes of the oil industry, but he'd been on the skids for a couple of years. He'd closed his office, fired his secretary and worked from home. Divorced with no kids, he lived alone.

The only promising bit of evidence came from his bank records. Ten days ago, he'd received fifty thousand dollars in an untraceable money transfer from a Swiss bank. Dormund had made large cash withdrawals that Jake assumed went to pay Granger.

The FBI hadn't been able to track the money or establish a link between Dormund and the COIN princes, but Jake had an investigative tool that they didn't. His old buddy Oscar was a successful attorney in Cheyenne who knew everybody and heard everything.

"I was wondering," Saida said, "if Maggie would enjoy coming to the ball."

He was one hundred percent certain that his sister would love flying on a private jet, and she'd been talking about seeing Oscar and his family. "Can you fix her up with something to wear?"

"Six suitcases," she reminded him.

"I'm pretty sure Maggie will like getting dolled up."

"Not like you?"

"Wearing a suit and shaking hands with politicians isn't my favorite thing, but that's part of the job. Just like those media briefings."

"You sound like Amir," she said. "He hates the politics but loves the work."

"Maybe your brother and I have a couple of things in common."

According to the directions on his GPS, they were getting close to Wade Freeman's ranch. A barbed-wire fence stretched along the side of the road. In a moonlit field, a herd of black Angus cattle were resting, some lying down and others upright.

Saida leaned forward to peer through the windshield. "The cows look so peaceful. They seem like friendly creatures."

"Cattle?"

"The sounds they make and the way they move. They're very docile beasts."

"Ever been close enough to smell a herd?"

Jake slowed at the turnoff to Freeman's ranch. The road was asphalt, nicely maintained with the weeds trimmed on both sides. The sprawling two-story house had flower beds across the front and a large vegetable garden to the right. A barn and other outbuildings were behind the main house.

According to the Freeman Ranch website, he ran over a thousand head of cattle. With an operation that large, he probably had a crew that lived here. In busy season, he was close enough to Dumont to hire part-time cowboys. There hadn't been any mention of a wife or children, but Wade Freeman had inherited the ranch from his mother who inherited from her family. Apparently, his mom kept her family name because this property had been called the Freeman Ranch for over seventy years.

Two men sat in rocking chairs on the well-lit wraparound porch. They both rose as Jake's police vehicle approached. After they parked, he and Saida got out of the car and strolled toward the porch.

He recognized Wade Freeman from the photos which really didn't do him justice. A tall rangy man with an easy smile, he came down the stairs from the porch to greet them as his companion went into the house. In spite of the white streaks in his black hair, he appeared to be only in his late thirties.

Jake spoke first. "Mr. Freeman, I'm Sheriff Jake Wolf. I apologize for coming by so late, but I had a couple of questions that wouldn't wait until morning."

The rancher gave him a firm handshake. "I voted for you."

"Thank you, sir."

Freeman turned his focus to Saida. "You're the princess from Jamala."

"I am."

He took her hand and raised it to his lips for a respectful kiss. "I'm glad to meet you."

Chapter Sixteen

Jake stood and stared. He'd never seen a cowboy kiss a lady's hand. Matter of fact, he'd never seen *anybody* do that. The courtly gesture was kind of nice, kind of classy. It'd be a damn shame if Wade Freeman turned out to be the money man who paid to have Saida attacked.

She responded gracefully to his hand-smooching with a slight inclination of her head. "It's a pleasure."

"Would you care to step inside? I could whip up some cocoa. We had apple pie for dessert, and there are leftovers."

Though Jake's mouth watered at the thought of pie and cocoa, he wanted to keep this conversation on a professional level. "No thanks. I'll just ask my questions, and we'll be on our way."

"Another time." He tilted his head up. "Beautiful night, isn't it? I never get tired of looking at those stars."

If Freeman had done anything criminal, he was doing an incredible job of covering up. He seemed like one of the most decent men Jake had ever met. With complete honesty, he said, "I'm sorry we haven't met before. Do you live here alone?"

"I don't have any family left, not since my mom passed away last year. There's a little apartment around back for the housekeeper and her little boy. And my foreman has a bedroom on the second floor. And I've got six full-time hands living in the bunkhouse."

That sounded just about right for a ranch this size. Jake was actually feeling guilty for bothering this man.

Freeman turned toward Saida. "I've heard many good things about you, Princess. Congratulations on completing your first year of law school."

"Thank you. May I ask how you knew I was in law school?"

"Your brother told me."

Surprise flashed in her eyes. "You've spoken to Amir?"

"Not recently." Freeman glanced toward Jake. "Believe me, Sheriff. If I knew where Amir was, I'd tell you in a heartbeat."

"Good to know."

Saida asked, "When did you make my brother's acquaintance?"

"A little over a year ago," Freeman said. "We made contact via the internet. You wouldn't think a rancher in Wyoming and a sheik from the Mediterranean would have much in common, but we share business interests."

"You raise cattle," she said. "I adore beef, but our people are mostly shepherds, goatherds and fishermen."

"Amir and I are both poking around the edges of the oil business, trying to make the right connections." Again, he looked toward Jake, including him in the conversation. "I've got over a hundred thousand acres, and my granddaddy wasn't a fool. The Freeman family owns the mineral rights. I'm researching my options."

Jake understood the reasoning. Freeman might be sitting on a fortune in untapped oil, but there were no guarantees. He could waste a lot of money on geological surveying and exploratory drilling. However, looking for advice from Amir was a strange move—a suspicious move.

"You contacted Amir about a year ago," Jake said. "Was that after your mother passed away?"

"You bet it was. Mom was opposed to oil prospecting on Freeman land."

And her son hadn't wasted any time furthering his own interests. Freeman's shiny bright first impression took on a bit of tarnish.

"What did you expect to learn from Amir?" Jake asked. "Your land holdings are different, the drilling process wouldn't be the same, and Amir doesn't have to deal with the American legal system."

"Money is the same all over the world," Freeman said. "Amir and I were dealing with some of the same investors and oil company people."

"I understand the need for research," Saida said. "In spite of his reputation for being impulsive, Amir invests a great deal of time in study before he makes a decision."

Freeman nodded. "That's why he set up this summit for the COIN nations. To make sure you're all on the same page."

"I wouldn't know," she said. "My brother didn't confide in me about the COIN summit. What do you know about it?"

"I was hoping to take part in a couple of meetings."

She paused for a moment, and Jake could see her thinking and calculating before she spoke. "Last year," she said. "My brother was in America on business. Did he visit you as a part of that trip?"

"That's right."

This was a big revelation—a huge chunk of the puzzle. For weeks, Jake had been trying to figure out why the royals had come here. "You're the reason Amir chose the Wind River Ranch and Resort for the COIN summit."

"It's more than that." Freeman gave an easy grin. "When Amir visited, he fell in love with Wyoming. He spent a lot of time by himself, exploring the territory and riding."

"Did he stay at your ranch?" she asked.

"Not for long, and he didn't want me to introduce him to anybody. He liked being anonymous. Not having bodyguards and pressures. Not having people watching his every move." He focused on Saida. "Being a princess, you must feel the same way at times."

"Only when I'm in Jamala," she said.

"You've been in the U.S. for a long time," he said. "Do you ever think about going back? Living in your home country?"

"It'd be difficult," she admitted. "In America, my horizons are wide open. In Jamala? No so much. But if Amir needed me, I'd go home."

"Would he admit that he needed you? He seems like a proud man who doesn't ask for help."

"That's true," she said. "He hardly ever shares his problems with me. He's too busy protecting me."

Jake couldn't believe his ears. This wasn't an interrogation. It was a damn therapy session. He needed to take control. "Mr. Freeman, you should have come forward with any information you had about Sheik Amir."

"Sorry, sheriff. I didn't mean to make your job harder. It's just that Amir wanted to keep our relationship quiet."

"And why is that?"

When Freeman shrugged, Jake sensed that their conversation had taken a sharp turn down a dark alley. Nice guy or not, Freeman was hiding something.

"You're going to have to give me a reason," Jake said. "Why does your relationship need to be secret?"

"Ranching is a simple lifestyle," he said. "It's hard for me to imagine all the complications of Amir's life. He's the ruler of a nation, dealing with political factions in Jamala as well as with the other island nations in COIN. He didn't want them to know he was talking to me."

"No, you're mistaken." Saida's reaction was sudden and

vehement. In an instant, she went from soft to tense. "Amir wouldn't keep secrets from the others. Efraim is like a brother to him."

"Don't get me wrong," Freeman said. "I'm not implying that Amir was suspicious or trying to put something over on the others. It's just a matter of timing."

Archly, she said, "Perhaps Amir didn't mention your relationship because you aren't as important as you think."

"Could be." Instead of taking offense, Freeman was gentle and conciliatory, almost apologetic. "When Amir disappeared, I wanted to help. I went over to the resort a couple of times and tried to introduce myself to the others."

A tidy explanation for why he'd appeared multiple times in Danny's photos. Everything Freeman said seemed reasonable, but Jake needed tangible proof. And an alibi.

He cut to the chase. "On the night Amir went missing, was he coming to see you?"

"No."

"Where were you that night?"

Freeman's affable smile slipped from his face. "I don't see why you want me to give you an alibi. I heard that the car was rigged with a bomb. I wouldn't have to be there to detonate the trigger."

The location where the explosion took place was nowhere near this ranch. It seemed unlikely that Amir was on his way here. "I'd still like an alibi."

"I was home. My foreman and my housekeeper can vouch for me."

Live-in employees came in handy. There wasn't much chance that they'd betray their boss. Jake tried a different tactic. "Your relationship with Amir might give me some insights to why he went missing. I'd like to see your correspondence with him."

"And I'd be happy to oblige," Freeman said, "just as soon as you show me a warrant."

Apparently, the friendly offers of pie and hand-kissing were over. Freeman shifted his posture, facing Jake in a direct confrontation. His face was stern. He wasn't exactly ordering them off his property, but the message was clear.

"Thanks for your time," Jake said. "I'll be back."

As he and Saida turned to leave, Freeman spoke to her, "Princess, if you need anything, please don't hesitate to contact me."

"My needs are well taken care of," she said.

He looked at her, then at Jake, then back at the princess again. His features relaxed. The smile returned to his face, and he gave Jake a wink.

IN THE CAR, SAIDA TURNED in her seat to look back at Freeman's ranch as they drove away. The two-story ranch house with lights shining on the porch and from one of the upstairs windows seemed as peaceful and calm as a picture postcard. When she thought of the West, this was the sort of scene she imagined—a moonlit ranch house with mountains in the background and cattle lowing from the field beside the road. If Freeman could be believed, Amir had been similarly enchanted by this countryside.

She didn't exactly know what to make of the rancher who claimed to know her brother. Supposedly, Freeman and Amir had a "relationship"—an odd word to describe a business association.

At first, she'd been drawn to Freeman, but she didn't like when he started casting aspersions. "He's wrong, you know. Efraim and the others would never betray Amir."

"It's the second time tonight that we've heard of trouble in the COIN paradise," Jake said.

"There are always enemies." She should have stayed in

closer touch with her brother, should have known who to suspect. "Our four small nations have a bond of loyalty. Of course, there are squabbles and disagreements, but I trust the princes more than a rancher who barely knows Amir."

"Freeman has secrets," Jake said. "The way he and Amir contacted each other seems suspicious."

"Are you going to get a warrant for his computer?"

"It's on my to-do list but not a top priority. My number one concern is solving the murder."

"And finding Amir," she reminded him.

"If we catch the killer, we'll find out who was after you. That person will lead us to your brother."

She appreciated the logic. With all these disparate bits of information bouncing around, it helped to have a clear vision. "How does Freeman fit into this picture?"

"I don't know that he does. I don't think Wade Freeman is a cold-blooded killer."

"How can you tell? Anyone could commit murder."

"Gut feeling," he said.

"That's not very practical."

"And it doesn't hold up in a court of law," he said. "But my gut is usually right. My impression of Freeman is that he's basically a decent man. He likes Amir. And he likes you."

His friendliness was undeniable. She wanted to like him, too. "He made me feel comfortable."

"By drooling on your hand?" He grinned. "That's a new one for me. When I started going to political events, I got used to the air kisses on both cheeks. But hand kissing?"

"I thought it was sweet." When Freeman raised her hand to his lips, she'd been surprised. But his attitude was perfectly respectable and reminded her of her brother. Amir had been known to woo the ladies with courtly gestures.

"What's the proper way to greet a princess?" he asked.

"It really doesn't matter."

He grinned. "A bow or curtsy? How about a fist bump? Or clicking your heels three times and spinning in a circle?"

"If you must know," she said, "there are ceremonial protocols for special occasions in Jamala. The greeting depends upon the position and rank of the individual. The lower the status, the deeper the bow."

"I'm guessing you wear costumes for your ceremonies, maybe a tiara or two."

She wasn't particularly fond of the formal events when she was required to wear royal robes and a ridiculous array of jewelry. "Are you teasing me?"

"Me? Hell, no. I'm just trying to figure out the right way to say hello to you."

She would have been annoyed if he hadn't been so appealing. He'd taken off his cowboy hat, and his black hair was handsomely disheveled. Two could play at this teasing game.

She unfastened her seat belt and leaned across the console to kiss his cheek. She whispered in his ear. "Here's my rule. When you greet me, you should be shirtless."

"What happens if I disobey?"

She nipped his earlobe. "I'll punish you."

"How?"

"I'll need to use your handcuffs." She gave him another little kiss and returned to her seat. "Where are we going now? To talk to the other person we saw in the photos? The guy who works for Maddox?"

"Give me a minute. I'm still thinking about you and me and handcuffs." He gave a shiver. "Okay, then. Right now, I'm taking you back to the resort."

When he mentioned the resort, she immediately thought of the luxurious suite and the bed with Italian linens. She'd like to sink into that bed with him, to make love until morning. "Will you stay with me?"

"I'd like nothing better than to spend the night with you, but not there. Not with Nasim and the royal entourage hovering outside the door."

Unfortunately, she agreed. The price she paid for being a royal was a lack of privacy. When she was in Jamala, her every move was scrutinized and judged. Even when she was a child, there were people watching her and Amir.

Her island homeland was so different from the vast, open terrain of Wyoming. Finding solitude in the mountains would be easy. When Amir had come here to visit Freeman, he'd gone off on his own. And now, he had disappeared again.

She gazed into the night, imagining her brother in a secluded mountain cabin, surrounded by peace and quiet. She imagined him safe and warm and happy. After he'd had enough time by himself, he would emerge. She would be united with him again. She had to believe that she'd find him.

Chapter Seventeen

Hoping to avoid running into the other royals, Saida directed Jake to the outdoor entrance for her suite. The landscaping at the Wind River Ranch and Resort was designed more for beauty than for security, but the ranch hands were working double duty as night watchmen. Jake exchanged a nod and a wave with a cowboy who sauntered across the grounds and around to the other side of the building.

She dug into her custom-made shoulder bag for the key to the privacy fence. Her Beretta was easily accessible, as was her cell phone, but the key card eluded her. She glared at the latch below the key card reader, and saw that the gate was open a crack.

Jake had also noticed. He whispered, "Was this locked when you left?"

She nodded.

"I'm going in," he said in a low voice. He took his gun from the holster and handed her the keys to his SUV. "Go back to the car."

She started to obey, retreating a few steps toward where they had parked. The SUV was several yards away. She heard a noise to her left, pivoted and peered into a neatly landscaped stand of aspen trees with the breeze rustling through the leaves.

Whirling again, she turned back toward the open gate.

Was the intruder still in her suite? Jake must think so; that had to be why he was being so quiet. Whether or not he wanted her there, she was going to provide backup for him.

Her gun fit neatly into her grasp. She dropped her purse just inside the gate so it wouldn't get in her way if she had to shoot. A shiver went through her. In target practice, she was extremely accurate, but she'd never fired her weapon at a living creature.

Moonlight shone on the hot tub and the flagstone terrace outside her room. The French doors were closed. Though the night was calm, it wasn't completely quiet. She heard the murmur of voices and laughter from another part of the resort.

As she watched, Jake turned the brass handle on the French door. It was open.

Now she was one hundred percent sure about the break-in. She might have absentmindedly left the gate unlocked, but not the door. She would have remembered to lock the door.

Before he stepped inside, he motioned for her to stay back. For a moment, she hesitated. She didn't want to distract him, but she didn't think she was any safer out here than in the room. Carefully, she crept toward the French doors.

From inside her room, she heard Jake curse. A light went on, and she hurried inside. A body was sprawled on the carpet beside her bed. From the blond ponytail, she identified Danny Harold.

Still holding his gun, Jake dropped to his knee beside Danny. One-handed, he shoved the photographer onto his back. The left side of Danny's forehead was matted with blood. He exhaled a low moan.

"He's alive," Jake said. "Call 911."

He wasted no more time with the fallen paparazzo. Jake moved quickly to check out the rest of the suite. Through the doorway, she saw the lights in the sitting room go on.

Since she'd left her purse with the cell phone outside, she went to the chair near the French doors and reached for the phone on the coffee table. As she pressed the button for the front desk, she noticed a scrap of lined paper on the table. In red pen, someone had written a phone number and three words: *Tell no one.*

Ever since she arrived in Wyoming, she'd been looking for evidence that would lead to her brother. And here it was—a red-lettered clue. She should give the scrap to Jake; his forensic team could process the clue, maybe find fingerprints.

But the message was clear. *Tell no one.* The person who had scribbled this note might have information that would lead to Amir. She had to do as instructed, couldn't risk telling Jake and putting her brother in more peril. She tucked the scrap into her jacket pocket.

The front desk picked up.

"This is Princess Saida." Her mouth was so dry that it was difficult to speak. "There's a badly injured man in my room. Call an ambulance."

"There's a nurse on the premises. Should I send her?"

"Immediately."

Jake returned to the bedroom with his cell phone in hand. "I contacted Wheeler," he said. "My people will be here soon."

"Did you find anything else?"

"Not that I can tell. Nothing seems out of place."

Having her possessions ransacked would have been preferable to finding that note. It burned in her pocket. She should tell Jake. They were working together. She trusted him.

Danny dragged himself to a sitting position. He touched his head and cringed. When his hand came away bloody, he stared at his fingers in shock. "What the hell?"

"Good question," Jake said. "Why were you in this room?"

"I'm injured." He looked at Saida. "It hurts."

"There's a medical person on the way," she assured him.

Jake grabbed Danny's arm and yanked him roughly to his feet. "Try not to bleed on the expensive furniture."

"Hey, I'm a person. I'm more important than a chair."

"That's debatable."

When Jake gave his arm a shake, Danny quivered all over. His legs wobbled like jelly. "Hurts," he repeated.

"Talk to me," Jake said. "How did you get into this room?"

Saida thought she might have the answer. "He was here earlier when he gave me the photos."

Jake jostled him again. "Did you swipe her key card?"

"Ow. Don't do that, man."

"Talk."

"Okay, maybe her key card fell into my camera bag. And maybe I came back here tonight to return it. Did you think of that, huh? I was doing the right thing."

"Yeah, sure," Jake said. "What time was it when you got here?"

"About an hour after dark. I came into the room and then..." he winced "...somebody came in behind me. Didn't see him until it was too late. Everything went black."

There was a knock at the outer door of the sitting room. Saida assumed it was the nurse. After Danny's confession, she didn't care if he was hurting. She was furious at him and, even more importantly, she desperately needed to know who had left the scrap of paper. "Did you recognize the man who hit you?"

"Just a blur." Danny's knees began to buckle. He sank toward the floor in slow motion. "I need something for this pain."

Jake hoisted him upright again. "Not until you tell me about this guy who attacked you. Was he short or tall?"

"Don't know."

"How about his clothes? What was he wearing?"

"Maybe jeans."

That was a safe call. Saida calculated that over half the men in Wyoming were habitually clad in denim.

"You had to see something," Jake said. "You were hit in the front of the head, facing your assailant."

"Didn't happen like that," Danny said. "He was behind me. I turned. Then, wham."

"Was he wearing a hat?"

"Yeah." Danny had a flash of coherence. "A baseball cap. It was red. And he had dark hair."

Jake prompted, "What did he say?"

"Nothing."

The knocking became more insistent, and Saida went to answer. She opened the door for a curly-haired woman in an EMT windbreaker and an angry-looking gentleman who introduced himself as the head of security for the resort.

Jake escorted Danny into the sitting room. "We found him in the bedroom. He'd stolen a key card."

The head of security clenched his jaw. "What should I do with him?"

"Treat his wound and hold him until one of my men gets here to accompany him to the hospital. He's under arrest." Jake gave Danny's arm another shake. "Do you hear that? You're under arrest for breaking and entering."

For once, Danny didn't have a comeback. Completely docile, he obeyed the EMT as she seated him in the wheelchair she had waiting in the hallway.

Jake stepped into the hall to quickly confer with the security head. "This room is a crime scene."

"Again." He scowled darkly.

"The forensic team will process the room as quickly as possible. They'll be discreet."

"Discretion is appreciated."

"After you're done with Danny, come back here," Jake said. "Until my men get here, I need your help."

"No problem, Sheriff."

Jake came back to her and closed the door to the room. "I'm afraid you won't be sleeping here tonight. Too bad. This place is incredible."

Earlier, she'd been thinking about sharing her luxurious bed with Jake. Not anymore. How could she sleep in a room with Danny's blood staining the carpet? How could she rest while the person who had left that note was still at large?

She ought to tell Jake. Now would be the right time.

Instead, she said, "I'll get my purse."

He followed her through the sitting room into the bedroom and outside onto the terrace where she found her purse exactly where she'd left it.

He stood beside the hot tub, admiring the shadowy view of distant peaks that reached high to touch the stars. With his thumbs hitched in his belt and his face tilted to catch the glow of moonlight, Jake was the iconic Western man—rugged, strong and unyielding. She trusted him. Even before she arrived in Wyoming, she trusted him. In her heart, she knew he was the man who would lead her to her brother.

She touched the pocket where she'd hidden the scrap of paper. *Tell him now.* But she couldn't. She wouldn't risk losing this tenuous thread that might lead her to Amir.

"What do you think he was after?" Jake asked.

Lost in her own dilemma, she mumbled. "Who? What?"

"We can assume that Danny wasn't looking for anything important to the investigation. He probably broke in to take pictures of your shoes. But the guy who attacked him was after something. Is there anything in your room that he'd want?"

"I had everything important with me." She held up her

purse. "I had my cell phone and my gun in my bag. My laptop is in your car."

"Think hard. Why would he sneak into your bedroom?"

To leave the red-lettered note. She made her decision. For now, she would say nothing to Jake. She'd play this clue alone.

Taking out her cell phone, she said, "I should inform Nasim about what happened. I know he's here at the resort. I saw the yellow Hummer."

"Don't make that call. Nasim is probably with the others. I want to tell them about the break-in at the same time. To see if anybody reacts."

"Surely, you don't think one of the royal entourage broke into my room."

"We'll see."

She knew that Jake was suspicious. He believed the seeds for all these attacks on COIN had originated in their native countries. But why would one of these men break into her room and leave a note for her to call him? It didn't make sense. None of this made sense.

AFTER THE HEAD OF SECURITY arranged for one of his men to guard the crime scene until a deputy arrived, he showed Jake and Saida to a conference room. Though the door was closed, she could hear a heated conversation taking place inside. She turned to the security man and asked, "How long have they been meeting?"

"An hour and twenty minutes," he said with a rueful smile. "It makes protecting them easier when they're all in one place."

"Who is in there?"

"The princes, Sheik Efraim, your bodyguard and four other people."

She straightened her shoulders and inhaled a deep breath.

Facing this group was like bearding a pride of ravenous lions. All strong men, they were leaders in their countries and were accustomed to being obeyed. They saw her as Amir's little sister who ran off to America and liked to have her picture taken on red carpets.

Her clothing didn't suit the occasion. Was there time to race back to her room and put on a serious, pinstriped suit that radiated power and confidence? Her jacket was too casual. She wasn't even wearing high heels.

Jake took her hand and squeezed. When she looked up at him, he gave her a nod. In his dark eyes, she saw encouragement. No matter what happened, Jake would be on her side.

She opened the door and stepped into the conference room. The long table surrounded by comfortable chairs had been abandoned. Everybody was standing.

Flanked by Prince Antoine and a bodyguard, Efraim angrily confronted Nasim. Using his long fingers, Efraim enumerated enemies to his nation.

Prince Stefan had distanced himself from the others. He stood at the wall of windows, peering into the darkness. One of his men was beside him.

The only person who acknowledged Saida's arrival was Callie who looked like she was about to explode. Her presence disturbed Saida. Even if Callie was Efraim's lover, her position as an assistant to the Secretary of Foreign Affairs could not be ignored. She shouldn't be a party to this COIN squabble.

Beside her, Jake stepped forward as though preparing to take charge of the situation. Though it was tempting to let him handle these problems, it wasn't right. This was her fight.

She touched his arm, signaling for him to hold back and wait. If she didn't make a statement now, she might as well accept her position as a window-dressing princess with no real power. Respect was not a right. Not for her, anyway. She had to command their attention.

Efraim ended his tirade by saying, "Your suspicion that anyone in my country was involved in Amir's disappearance is absurd."

Prince Stefan Lutece said, "It's an insult."

"Look to your own country," Efraim said. "Not everyone in Jamala wanted Amir to rise to power."

Saida stepped forward and slammed both palms on the tabletop. "Listen to me."

The room went silent. Heads turned. She felt their eyes staring at her.

Proudly, she said, "I will speak for my brother. And for the people of Jamala."

Chapter Eighteen

Jake had been impressed by Saida's performance in that conference room. She'd been strong and smart and regal as all hell. With a couple of reasonable statements, she'd ended the bickering and gotten the royals to sit around the table. She'd put those boys in their place.

When she announced that her room had been broken into, he'd watched their reactions and saw expressions of surprise, anger and frustration. Nobody had looked guilty.

Then, Saida tactfully suggested that he and Callie leave the room. There was COIN business to discuss.

In the hallway, he stood beside Callie. They were a little bit uncomfortable with each other. Jake had been obliged to arrest her younger brother when the kid got himself tangled in the royal intrigues and ended up shooting a man. As it turned out, though the young man's motives had been decent, he'd still have to stand trial. The law was the law.

Callie cleared her throat. "I'm glad that Saida agreed to attend the ball in Cheyenne."

"I'm going, too."

"As her escort?"

"It's more political," he said. "I got a phone call from the attorney general. He wanted me to show up and assure everybody that we have things under control."

"Do you?"

That was a question he'd rather not answer. He changed the subject. "Your family has lived around here a long time. What do you know about Wade Freeman?"

"The rancher?"

Jake nodded. "Tall guy. He has some silver in his hair but I'm guessing he's not over forty."

"Kind of a loner," she said. "I seem to recall that he was married in his twenties, and his wife died in a car accident. He didn't marry again, but the rumor is that he and his house-keeper might be hooking up." She cocked her head to one side. "Why are you interested in him?"

"There's a possible connection to Amir."

"Of course there is." She didn't bother to disguise the bitterness in her voice. "I'll be glad when this is over. When you became sheriff, you probably didn't expect anything like this."

"No, I didn't." That had to be the heaviest understatement of his life.

"Big Burt Maddox is making a lot of noise about how you aren't experienced enough to handle the situation."

"What do you think?"

She gave him a half grin. "The smart money is on you, Sheriff. You're going to do all right."

He wondered if she was talking from a political perspective or a personal one. Callie had connections in government. She knew a thing or two about politics and could probably school him on the right way to behave at the ball.

But that wasn't an in-depth conversation he wanted to have right now. He excused himself and returned to Saida's suite.

The head of security had posted himself outside the door. He gave Jake a nod. "Your people are here. Anything I can do?"

"I'll let you know."

Inside the suite was the organized chaos typical of most crime scenes. Wheeler and four other uniformed deputies were in the sitting room, shuffling their feet and looking around as though a clue might jump out and grab them around the throat.

Another night with overtime. If Jake checked the parking lot, he'd probably see every vehicle owned by the sheriff's department. It was going to take a sheik's ransom to meet his payroll this month.

He turned to Wheeler. "Are the forensics people here?"

"Jane's in the bedroom taking prints. She's got a couple of assistants with her."

Jake addressed the other deputies. "Thanks for responding. You're all dismissed until your regular shifts. Exit through the door to the lobby."

As they left, he heard grumbling. No doubt a couple of these guys were complaining about how Maddox would have handled this crime scene better. They might be correct. Jake felt like he was losing control, running in circles.

He got Wheeler headed in a productive direction. "I want you to interview witnesses. As far as we know, the intruder entered the suite from the outside. He might have gone out the same way or he might have exited through the lobby area. His description is vague. We're looking for a male, average height and weight, possibly wearing a red baseball cap."

Wheeler took out his little spiral notebook. "Do you want me to knock on doors? Wake people up?"

Jake's cop instinct was to interview everybody as soon as possible. The politics of being sheriff told him otherwise. He needed to maintain good relations with the Wind River Ranch and Resort—a major employer in the area. Their guests were paying big bucks for the privilege of staying here, and these people had already been inconvenienced several times.

"First, question the employees. Coordinate all your interviews with the security man outside. Unless it's absolutely necessary, don't wake up a bunch of innocent people."

"Copy that, Sheriff."

Jake watched as Wheeler went into the hallway. His deputy was proving himself invaluable. When this mess was over and the dust settled, Wheeler was getting a promotion. Some of the complainers would be getting the boot.

In the bedroom, he found the CSIs taking photos and dusting for prints. The forensics expert, Jane Cameron, was on her hands and knees, dabbing at the bloodstain on the carpet. She scrambled to her feet when she saw Jake. "Over here, Sheriff. I've got something to show you."

He couldn't help but notice how sparkly she was. Her brown hair was shiny, her eyes gleamed and her teeth flashed. Falling in love with Prince Stefan had turned up her wattage.

Standing over the glass-topped coffee table, Jane pointed to a distinct fingerprint. "This might be worth something."

One lousy print didn't mean much. In a place like this where staff and guests were constantly coming and going, there tended to be a lot of extraneous trace evidence. "Why is that print so important?"

"This place is clean." She gestured widely to encompass the whole room. "I mean, it's super clean. The maids must be wiping down the surfaces two or three times a day. That print is the only one I found on any of the tables or dressers."

He pointed to the French doors. "What about there? On the frame and the windows?"

"Several fingerprints. I assume some of them are yours and Saida's."

"That's right," he said. "Did you find anything else on the terrace?"

"No apparent footprints. Since the lock wasn't picked, there weren't any scratches in the wood. Don't worry, Sheriff. I'll have all the evidence for you by tomorrow morning."

"Call me if you have anything before then."

He stepped aside and let her do her job. The evidence gathering was underway, and he was confident in the abilities of his team. His responsibility, at this point, was to put the pieces together and come up with a coherent answer.

Leaving the suite, he paced down the hall to the lobby, passed the bar and exited through the front doors. The entry was well lit, as was the parking lot, but he didn't have to go far to find darkness and quiet.

He followed an asphalt path that meandered through the mowed, landscaped grounds of the resort. The outdoors was where he did his best thinking.

His first logistical question concerned timing. If Danny, the idiot paparazzo, could be believed, he'd entered using the key card. The intruder came in behind him and knocked Danny unconscious.

Had the intruder known of Danny's plan? Had he followed Danny with the express intention of using him to get into Saida's suite? Jake wouldn't be surprised to learn that Danny had bragged about having a private meeting with the princess. He could easily imagine the paparazzo at one of the local taverns, puffing out his scrawny chest and talking about how he and the princess were great friends. But would he mention the key card? Not even Danny was stupid enough to reveal his plans for breaking and entering.

That meant the intruder had already been in place, watching the resort and waiting until nightfall to make his move. With the ranch hands on patrol as night watchmen, the window of opportunity for making a break-in was narrow.

Danny said he'd showed up just after dark. His arrival—coincidence or not—had saved the intruder a lot of trouble and risk.

The bigger question was motive. Why had the intruder broken into Saida's suite? She hadn't made a thorough search of her belongings, but nothing seemed to be disturbed. And this intrusion wasn't a simple robbery.

Had he been looking for information? She'd had her cell phone and laptop with her, and that might have foiled his search. What was he after?

Jake paused on the pathway and gazed up at the North Star, wishing for strength. He turned to the east and the south. If legends were true, the stars should have spelled out the answers to his questions. But there was no magic in the night sky.

He had to figure it out for himself.

In his mind, he turned the question of motive around and around. A break-in occurred. Nothing was taken.

Maybe something had been left behind.

But what?

The intruder could have come into Saida's rooms and planted a tiny camera or a listening device to spy on her. A foolish idea. Jake could have the rooms swept for bugs and spy cams.

Frankly, he didn't want Saida to stay in that room anymore. Yes, the resort was beautiful and luxurious. Security had been breached. To make sure she'd be safe, he needed to take her home with him. He wanted her to share his bed.

His motivation didn't have a damn thing to do with security or the investigation. His desires were irresponsible, inappropriate. And he didn't care. He wanted to make love to the princess.

Quickly, he returned to the resort and went to the conference room. The door was still closed, but it was going to take more than a slab of wood to stop him. Jake tapped on the wood and waited.

Nasim answered. Though his eyelids drooped with exhaustion, his suit was still impeccable and his necktie still knotted neatly.

"I need to speak with Princess Saida," Jake said. "About the investigation."

The old man opened the door wider and beckoned to Saida. As soon as she saw him, she grabbed her purse and rushed away from the conference table toward him. To the others, she said, "I'll be back shortly."

Jake's heart jumped when he saw her eagerness. It took an effort to keep from smiling. "I have a few questions. Come with me."

In the hallway leading to the lobby, she fell into step beside him. "I'm so glad you rescued me. I was about to faint from boredom."

"The talk isn't going well?"

"Oh, it's going great. I've heard more about oil drilling and COIN political factions than I ever wanted to know."

He wanted to be alone with her, but the princess was an attention magnet. One of the women working at the front desk had moved away from her post to get a better view of Saida.

Might as well use that interest. Jake approached the curious woman and asked, "Is there a place where the princess and I can speak privately?"

She went through a half-curtsy dance similar to the way Maggie had first greeted the princess, then she directed them to an office behind the desk, giggled and closed the door.

Jake knew he shouldn't touch Saida. If they were found in an embrace, there'd be no end of trouble. But she was worth it. He caught hold of her waist. Slowly, he reeled her toward him. Her hands glided up his chest and wrapped around his neck. Her body fit against him like a velvet glove.

It felt good to hold her, damn good.

He lowered his head and whispered in her ear, "You can't stay in your suite tonight."

"I know. It's a crime scene."

"Come home with me."

Her head tilted back and she looked up at him with eyes so warm that he began to melt. "I want to, Jake. I really do. But I can't leave. Not now. I've finally gotten these guys to trust me."

Having dealt with the royals, he knew what an amazing accomplishment it was to have them change their minds. "I'm proud of you."

"It was your idea. You were the one who suggested that someone from Jamala or another COIN nation might have financed Dormund and Granger."

He liked that she was still investigating. Her focus on finding Amir overwhelmed everything else. "What have you found out?"

"I'm not sure that you're right. We need a clue. Something that would…"

Her words trailed off, and her body tensed. Something was bothering her. "What is it, Saida?"

"Nothing." But her smile turned stiff. "Why don't you want me to stay in the suite?"

"Logic. Since the intruder didn't steal from you, I think he broke into your room to leave something. It might be some kind of spy cam."

She buried her face in the crook of his neck and held him tightly for a long moment. Then she broke away.

"You're right, Jake. He left something. A message. It was in plain sight on the coffee table by the phone." She dug into her pocket and took out a scrap of paper with red lettering. "A phone number and a warning. It says that I should tell no one."

Not even him. She should have known better than to withhold evidence. "What were you thinking?"

"I was afraid. I didn't want to risk losing a connection that would lead to my brother."

"Have you made the call?"

She shook her head. "I didn't want to do anything until I talked to you."

Though he wished she would have instinctively handed the note to him the minute she found it, he appreciated her trust—belated though it was. He took a backward step and leaned against the desk. "Go ahead. Call him."

She took her cell phone from her purse and punched in the number. For over a minute, she held the phone to her ear. She disconnected and tried again.

He could feel her tension rising. Avoiding his gaze, she paced in front of the desk. She tried again. And again. "Why won't he answer? I don't understand."

"Give me the phone number. I'll run a trace. I can find out who it belongs to."

"No," she said firmly. "I trust you, Jake. Trust you with my life. But I don't want anyone else knowing about this note or this phone number."

It wasn't her decision. She didn't get to call the shots when it came to evidence. That was his job, and he had a responsibility to do things right. The correct procedure would be for him to confiscate the note so forensics could check for fingerprints. But he also needed her cooperation, especially now that she'd been accepted into the inner circle of the COIN royals.

Her gaze met his. Sadly, there was a distance. The heat between them had chilled by several degrees. She was using their relationship to circumvent police procedure. And he was using her, as well.

"Promise me one thing," he said. "You won't call that number without telling me."

"Done."

For now, that would be enough.

Chapter Nineteen

The next morning at a few minutes before seven o'clock, Saida awoke with a start. Yanked from slumber, she reached for the cell phone on the bedside table. The number—scrawled in red ink—flashed in her brain. Last night, she'd made two more attempts to reach the intruder. Both times, Jake had been standing by, watching while she placed the call.

No one had answered.

Maybe this morning, maybe now, she'd have better luck.

She dragged herself from the bed. Though her new room at the resort was far less luxurious than her original suite, the bed linens were soft as a caress. Under normal circumstances, she would have allowed herself to glide into a new day, reveling in the drowsy warmth of the comfortable bed and ordering espresso from room service. Not today.

She called Jake's house on the landline in the room. When he answered, his voice was husky and warm. She wondered if he was still in his bed. More important, would she ever share that bed?

Last night, he'd been angry with her for not telling him right away when she found the note. In the blink of an eye, he'd transformed from hot, sexy lover to super-responsible sheriff. He was still hot and sexy, of course. That was his natural state of being.

"Did I wake you?" she asked.

"I'm up."

"And dressed?"

"I just got out of the shower."

She closed her eyes, conjuring a mental image of Jake wearing nothing but a skimpy bath towel around his waist.

"Saida, why did you call?"

She exhaled a sigh as her fantasy dissipated. "I thought I'd try the mystery number again."

"Go for it," he said. "Remember what we discussed."

"I remember." Last night, he'd given her a few guidelines for handling a telephone negotiation with a criminal. First, she needed to remember that bad guys lied and shouldn't be believed. Second, her goal was to get as much information as possible, asking where he was and if she could meet with him face-to-face. Third, she shouldn't agree to anything.

"Call him on your cell," Jake said. "I'll be right here, listening."

From memory, she punched in the red-lettered number and listened while it rang several times. Why wouldn't he answer? This person had gone to a great deal of trouble and had taken a risk to leave his number in her room. Where was he?

She disconnected. "No answer."

"Don't let it shake you," he said.

"What kind of game is he playing?" Tension gripped her by the throat. Finally, she had a clue, a connection, a person who might lead her to Amir. Why wouldn't he pick up his phone? "It's making me crazy."

"He'll answer when he's ready. In the meantime, we have a lot to do."

"Such as?"

"Much as I hate to get involved in girl stuff, Maggie has

been bouncing off the wall ever since I told her she'd be coming to the ball. She needs to talk about clothes with you."

"Our plane leaves at four o'clock. I'll see Maggie before then."

"Much appreciated," he said. "Later today you and I can interview the other people who showed up repeatedly in Danny's photos. There's the guy who works for Maddox, his name is Chuck Scowron. And the lady who owns the quilt shop."

"I'll be at your office by nine," she said.

THOUGH SHE DIDN'T WASTE a moment, it took longer than expected for her to deal with the morning's business. At a few minutes after ten o'clock, Nasim drove the yellow Hummer into the parking lot for the county courthouse in Dumont.

Saida hadn't spent much time in the town and decided that she hadn't missed much. Dumont was pleasant but unremarkable, and the courthouse had all the charm and architectural elegance of a beige brick shoebox.

As Nasim guided the car into an empty space, she said, "You really don't have to accompany me."

"Until our departure this afternoon, I will act as your bodyguard. It is my duty."

He wasn't altogether pleased with the plan for him to return to Jamala and take a stronger leadership role with the bickering factions. And he definitely didn't like being pushed into that position by the COIN royals.

"I'll be fine," she assured him.

"You must not underestimate the threat, Princess."

"I assure you, Nasim, I'm taking all that has happened very seriously." She knew the potential for danger existed. Not just for her, but for Amir. "I won't take any risks."

"You are impatient," he said.

"But I get things done. Did you ever think I'd get the

princes to listen to me? They wouldn't let me leave this morning. Even Efraim had to admit that I had insight."

"I have said many times, you are a born diplomat. And your brother is a statesman. Together, you are formidable."

On the second floor, they went down a wide hallway to a pair of double doors where the sheriff's department was located. Inside, she and Nasim approached a wood counter that separated the entryway from a large room with partitions, desks, file cabinets and office equipment.

Through a half-glass wall, she could see Jake in his office. He was talking to Deputy Wheeler.

The middle-aged woman who occupied the desk directly in front of Jake's office did a double take when she looked up and saw Saida and Nasim. In this very functional office, Saida knew that they stood out. Nasim's tailored suit, white shirt and necktie seemed as formal as a tuxedo. Though she'd dressed casually, her gray slacks had a designer shimmer, her blouse was purple silk and her four-inch platform heels were embellished with red leather stars.

The woman bustled toward them, peering over the rims of her silver-frame glasses. Her mouth pursed in a tight little bow as though she was holding back words.

Saida made the first move, stepping forward to grasp the woman's hand and give a firm shake. "I'm Saida. This is Nasim. We're here to see the sheriff."

"I'm Jake's secretary. Maggie told me all about you, Princess." Her smile lingered on Nasim. "But she didn't mention this gentleman. Are you a sheik, too?"

"I am Minister of Affairs for Jamala," he said.

"Affairs, eh? That sounds mighty interesting. We might need to chat about affairs." She gestured for them to follow her. "The sheriff is expecting you."

Jake's private office was relatively small and blah. In addition to the desk and chairs, there was a basketball hoop and a couple of photos—one of which showed a school picture of young men in light blue-and-red basketball uniforms. As soon as Saida entered, she was hit by the urge to decorate. This room needed to be more personalized. Until Jake put his own stamp on his office, he hadn't really settled into his position.

After she greeted Wheeler, Saida was anxious to make her next attempted phone call to the mystery number. "I need to speak to the sheriff in private," she said. "Perhaps Deputy Wheeler could show Nasim where to find coffee."

As soon as they left the office, she whipped out her cell phone. "Can I try again?"

"Sit." He pointed to a chair on the opposite side of his desk. "I have some information."

"Good news?" She perched on the edge of the chair.

"I have the preliminary forensics report from Jane Cameron regarding your suite at the resort. She found a fingerprint on the coffee table near the windows."

"Which is where I found the note," she said. "Who is it?"

"Not so fast." He laced his fingers behind his head and tilted back in his chair. "I'd like to take this opportunity to mention that this information is the result of simple, old-fashioned police work. Open and direct."

"You've made your point."

"Have I?" He stared up at the ceiling. "Over the past few weeks, I've put up with a wall of silence from the COIN entourage. They've withheld information and evidence. On occasion, they've refused to cooperate."

"I'm not like them," she protested.

His hands separated and he leaned across the desk toward her. "Last night, your first instinct was to hide that note."

"And my second instinct was to tell you." She stood and rested her palms on the desk. "When I came to Wyoming, your house was my first stop. I came to you. Not the princes."

He stood, facing her. "No secrets, Saida."

"Tell me who left the phone number, Jake."

"The fingerprint was from Chad Granger."

As soon as he said the name, it seemed obvious. Granger tried to abduct her. The dead man was found in Granger's truck. "What do you think he wants from me?"

Jake shrugged. "Try the number again."

She dialed and listened to the monotonous drone of the ringer. Once, twice, three times…

"Nothing," she said.

Jake looked worried. "I can think of only one reason Granger would contact you. He wants money."

"A ransom." She was immediately on edge. The thought of Amir being held captive was terrible. At least she'd know that he was alive. "I'd pay anything to rescue my brother."

"It's doubtful that somebody like Granger could pull off a kidnapping," he said. "I think he wants to sell you information."

"I'd pay. Why won't he answer?"

When she looked into Jake's eyes, she saw the dark possibility that neither of them wanted to say aloud. Granger might not be able to pick up his phone. He might already be dead.

Wheeler tapped on the office door and pushed it open. "Sorry to interrupt, Sheriff. But we've got a lead on Dormund's rental car."

"Where is it?" Jake asked.

"In the mountains west of town. A couple of hikers called it in. They spotted a vehicle that apparently drove off a cliff. The license plate matches the one we have for Dormund."

"Did they climb down and take a look inside?"

"Yes, sir."

She could hear her heart thumping. The last time they'd found a vehicle, it was the truck, and William Dormund was dead. Would the rental car tell the same story? She feared that Granger had been killed before she could talk to him.

"Was anyone in the car?" Jake asked.

"The hikers saw blood on the driver's side, but no body."

Saida never thought she'd be glad to hear a statement like that. *Blood but no body.* For the moment, as far as she knew, Granger was still alive, and he might be able to sell her information that would lead to her brother.

She sat back in the chair and watched as Jake efficiently organized the next step in the investigation. He dispatched Wheeler and two other deputies to follow up on the hiker's statement. After they located the wreck, they should do a preliminary search.

If there was any indication that the driver might have crawled away from the crash and might still be in the area, Wheeler should contact the mountain rescue team to search, and then arrange for the car to be towed to the impound lot.

Wheeler looked up from the spiral notebook where he was writing as fast as he could. "Whoa there, Sheriff. Who do I call at mountain rescue?"

Jake rattled off a name and phone number. "Call me when you get to the scene."

"How can I tell if the driver got away from the wreck?"

"First, you have to determine if the driver was in the car when it went over the edge. There should be tire marks if he tried to stop. Look for a blood trail. It hasn't rained so there could be footprints." Jake paused. "You know what, I'm coming with you. It'll be good for me to do some field work."

"Good idea." Wheeler flipped his notebook closed.

"Don't look so happy," Jake said. "We have a press briefing at eleven. That's going to be your job."

"Me? I don't know what to tell them."

"You've heard me do this often enough." Jake clapped

him on the shoulder. "There are only two words you need to know. No comment."

"But Sheriff, I'm not—"

"Handle it. That's an order." He turned to Saida. "I'm going to be tied up for the rest of the day. I'll meet you at the airfield at four."

"What about my phone calls?"

"Keep trying."

He touched her arm. His gaze met hers. For an instant, she thought he meant to kiss her. But he only smiled.

There should have been something she could say to him, some way she could tell him how important he was to her. She admired the way he took charge. The citizens of Wind River County didn't appreciate what a good job he was doing. Truly, there was nothing sexier than a man who had found his calling and performed his job well.

Chapter Twenty

At ten minutes until four o'clock, Nasim drove the Hummer onto the tarmac beside the main hangar at the private airfield on the outskirts of Dumont. Saida rode in the front seat. Sheik Efraim and Callie were in the back. Efraim wasn't coming with them to Cheyenne; he was escorting Callie—a duty that apparently included kissing and holding hands when they thought Saida wasn't looking. And he would drive the Hummer back to the resort.

Earlier this afternoon, Saida had spent some time with Maggie and they'd picked out a simple toga-style gown in a soft peach color that emphasized her glowing skin tone. Finding the proper shoes was more difficult; Maggie's feet were a size larger than hers. They decided on a pair of open-toed sandals with jeweled straps.

Most of Saida's day had been occupied with learning the names of various investors and politicians. Furthering the oil industry in the COIN nations seemed like a petty concern until Nasim reminded her that Amir hoped to ensure a prosperous future for Jamala through their natural resources. Amir would want her to handle this well.

Her brain was overloaded with names and connections, but as she disembarked from the Hummer, she held only one important thought: Jake. Last night, he had very nearly propositioned her when he suggested that she stay with him. She was ready. Tonight at the hotel, she would say yes, yes, yes.

This trip to Cheyenne was the perfect opportunity for Jake to be less responsible than usual. He'd be free from the constant scrutiny in Dumont, and there would be no midnight calls regarding his duties. Not like today.

He'd spent several hours at the crime scene with the wrecked rental car. The rest of the time, he was coordinating the many facets of the investigation. He was an amazing sheriff. Of that, she was sure. In his realm—Wind River County—he was brilliant.

She wished that she was more comfortable in his world. Being a princess didn't prepare her for life in a small town where everyone tried to fit in. She was foreign. She stood out. Always had, always would. There would always be those who resented her and those who outright disliked her.

To be completely honest, she didn't think Jake could transition into her world, either. Jamala was a sunny island where his cowboy boots would be a joke, and the citizens would be dismayed to find she was involved with an American.

The same might be true of the rarified, sophisticated atmosphere of Beverly Hills. Jake was too real, too natural. She didn't see him as someone who would shine on a red carpet. A long-term relationship with him seemed impossible; she would have to be satisfied with one night, maybe two.

As she approached the sleek private jet, she saw Maggie talking to the pilot. Jake must already be here. Soon they'd be together. Though it was ridiculous to miss him after being apart for only a few hours, she was anxious and excited.

He stepped from the plane's interior onto the staircase and stood there. In his black suit and white shirt with the collar open, he was as handsome as a movie star, definitely worthy of any red carpet. The only hint of Wyoming was his wolf belt buckle. Subtly, she lifted her cell phone and took a picture.

When he smiled at her, she was struck by the perfect symmetry of his white teeth and high cheekbones. Beverly Hills would love this man. He was gorgeous enough to fit in anywhere.

After he greeted her and Callie, he helped load their luggage into the cargo hold. "Only two suitcases? Saida, you're traveling light."

"What did you bring?"

He pointed to a gym bag. "I wouldn't have needed that much, but I have a change of shoes in case I get time to shoot hoops with Oscar."

Maggie joined them. "I can't wait to see Oscar. I love his family, and he might be about to hook me up with a job in Cheyenne."

Saida asked, "If you leave, who will take care of your brother?"

"Jake's a big boy," Maggie said. "He'll manage."

"Oscar wants you to work in his office," Jake said. "He thinks you'd make a better lawyer than a shrink."

"Well, I'll just have to show him how wrong he is."

She flounced up the stairs to enter the plane, and the rest of them followed. Though Saida was accustomed to first-class travel, she appreciated the luxury of a private jet. The eight seats in the cabin were comfortable, arranged in two sections with a table with two chairs on each side. She and Jake were side by side, facing Callie and Maggie.

Nasim settled into a seat by himself. He reclined the seat and closed his eyes. After they reached Cheyenne, he would be continuing his journey back to Jamala. An arduous trip. He needed his rest.

When they were airborne, Maggie flipped open her laptop. "Is it okay for me to use this?"

"Not a problem." Saida showed her how to connect to the internet.

"There's something I wanted to read to you," Maggie said. "It's a blog from someone who calls herself the Lipstick Lady, and it's one of the first things that pops up when I type Jake's name into the search box."

He leaned back and groaned. "Is this necessary?"

Callie said, "It's good to know what you're stepping into."

"I know," he said. "It's a big, steaming pile of—"

"Here it is," Maggie said brightly. "The headline is 'Sexy Sheriff Meets Pouty Princess.'"

"Pouty?" Saida took offense. "I'm not pouty."

"Here's what it says." Maggie read from the blog. "'Those of you who have been following the daily news briefings from Dullsville, Wyoming, have no doubt fallen madly in love with Sheriff Jake Wolf, known as the Wolfman when he played basketball. Sorry to report that it's too late for us mere mortals. Sheriff Jake—a manly man if I ever saw one—is having a fling with none other than the fashion icon from Jamala, Princess Saida Khalid. The princess has had dozens of dudes, including half of the Lakers. I'm calling a foul. Why can't she leave Jake for the rest of us?'"

It was Saida's turn to groan. "I'd like to make it clear that I only dated two of the Lakers. And nothing happened."

"I'm still impressed," Jake murmured. "It's not a bad thing to be linked with the Lakers."

"This Lipstick blogger makes it sound like I was having sex with the whole team."

"If I was a lawyer," Maggie said, "I'd sue for slander."

"Libel," Callie corrected. "Slander refers to spoken defamation. Libel is for written. And it would mean a long, protracted, expensive court battle."

"I know," Maggie said. "Jake was always cool about the lies they printed when he was running for sheriff. I hated it, especially when they called him a drunken Indian. I'm sure Burt Maddox was behind those stories."

"Burt lost," Jake said. "I won. End of story."

Saida didn't enjoy notoriety, but she accepted the rumors as part of her duty as princess. No matter what was said about her, mentions in the press brought attention to Jamala.

"The story about you two having an affair is going to pick up steam," Callie said, "especially when you show up together at the Cattlemen's Ball. There will be photos and innuendos, whether it's true or not."

Jake turned to her and lifted an eyebrow. "Maybe we should give them something to talk about."

She wouldn't mind turning their rumored affair into reality, wouldn't mind at all. "Maybe we should."

WHILE THE LADIES WERE getting dressed at the hotel, Jake took the opportunity to meet Oscar Pollack for dinner at the hotel restaurant—a white tablecloth place with a menu that ranged from escargot to hamburger. His old friend was obviously doing well, brimming with the confidence he had lacked when they'd first met ten years ago. He was tanned and fit, and he'd shaved his head since the last time Jake saw him.

"Cue ball," Jake said. "I like it."

"So does my wife."

They ordered dinner—grilled rib eye for Jake and a T-bone for Oscar—and caught up on what was happening with Oscar's family. He seemed genuinely enthused about hiring Maggie to work at his office. "I need an admin," he said. "She's smart and polite but won't put up with any guff."

"She needs to earn some cash this summer. The phrase 'starving college student' is more than a metaphor."

"You don't need to remind me." Oscar had worked his way through college and law school. He took a sip of his lemonade, regarded Jake critically and said, "Tell me about your investigation."

When Jake started talking, the words spilled out in a torrent. It was a relief to discuss the ins and outs of what had happened since the COIN royals came to Wind River County, and it was a long story. By the time Jake had caught up to the present, they'd had a refill on lemonade and their steaks had arrived.

"Today," he said, "I checked out the wrecked rental car. My preliminary conclusion is that it was pushed over the edge of the cliff to dispose of it."

"Nobody in the car?"

"If there was a driver, he jumped before the car went over. There were bloodstains on the driver's seat, and the blood type matches William Dormund. It's likely that he was murdered in the car, and then his body was moved to where we found it."

"Did you find fingerprints on the vehicle?"

"My forensic people haven't had it long enough to make a report." Jake cut into his steak. A beautiful piece of meat, it oozed juice. "But I found something else in the trunk. A Beretta that belongs to the princess."

Oscar made the immediate connection. "The gun that was stolen from her luggage. I assume you filed a missing weapon report when she knew it was gone."

"I did," he said. "I'm pretty sure ballistics will show that her gun fired the bullet that killed Dormund. I know she's not guilty. She was at my house when Dormund was shot. But having her weapon used in the murder looks bad. It ties her to the crime and suggests that she knows the killer."

"A lame attempt to incriminate her."

"Very lame."

"Big picture," Oscar said. "Amir is still missing. The bad guys want to find him, and they attempted to kidnap Saida so they could use her as leverage or because they think she knows where her brother is hiding."

"These so-called bad guys paid Dormund and Granger to do their dirty work."

"And you're assuming the bad guys are associated with a political faction in one of the COIN nations—people who would benefit by having Amir out of the way."

"Maybe."

For a moment, they ate in silence. Jake had the feeling that his friend had information that might be useful but was hesitant about talking. Oscar was a lawyer, after all. He had to be discreet.

"I didn't know Dormund well," he said, "and I don't generally traffic in rumor. But I have reason to believe that he had connections that were closer to home, not all the way around the world in Jamala."

"I'm listening."

"Dormund was a lawyer before he was disbarred and became a private eye. He had a gambling problem, lost a lot of money on the ponies." Oscar hesitated again. "Did you check his client list?"

"The FBI went through his records. His file-keeping system was a mess. And we never located his computer."

"Maybe you've heard," Oscar said, "Burt Maddox's wife is living in Cheyenne."

"She's here taking care of her parents, right?"

"And getting away from her husband. She's been talking to divorce lawyers. Some of those lawyers might have used the services of Dormund to investigate Big Burt."

"I don't suppose you could give me the names of these lawyers," Jake said.

"You don't need their names." Oscar sliced off a thick chunk of T-bone. "The important thing is the connection between Maddox and Dormund."

Maddox had been creeping around the edges of his investigation. He'd found the truck and pointed them toward Granger. Both Maddox and one of his men had made it a point to hang around at the resort. Big Burt Maddox always bragged that nothing went on in Wind River County that he didn't know about. Jake might be wise to focus on him as a suspect.

Jake checked his wristwatch. It was almost seven o'clock. "I should go upstairs and see if the ladies are ready. They said seven, but I'm not counting on it."

A huge grin slid across Oscar's face. "Tell me all about the princess."

"She's beautiful. Has a good sense of humor. And she's smart, in her second year at UCLA law school."

He chuckled. "It's been a real long time since I've seen that goofy look on your face. You like her. You like her a lot."

"Maybe."

Jake looked toward the front of the restaurant. Saida was talking to the maître d', and he was bowing repeatedly. She spotted Jake and waved.

"There she is," he said.

Oscar turned in his seat. "Wow."

Her deep purple gown was strapless, displaying a lot of skin and a necklace with an emerald-colored stone the size of a traffic light. As she made her way through the tables, conversations stopped and people stared.

Jake rose to greet her. In her formal dress, she looked like royalty. Not only that, she was wearing some kind of crown in her hair. There was only one way he felt like he could properly greet her.

He took her hand, raised it to his lips and brushed a light kiss over her knuckles. "Princess, I'd like you to meet Oscar Pollack."

Oscar was gaping. Not a problem for Saida, she gave him a warm hug. "I've heard so much about you."

"Princess," he said.

"I just came down here to tell Jake that we're ready. If we don't leave soon, Maggie is going to explode with excitement."

Oscar swallowed hard and recovered his poise. "We'll have more time to talk at the ball. My wife wanted to know if she's supposed to curtsy when she meets you."

"Tell her I like a fist bump."

Saida linked her arm with Jake's, and they sailed out of the restaurant.

Chapter Twenty-One

When their limousine pulled up in front of Little America, Jake exited the car first. He'd been to other events at this hotel—political fundraisers and dinners. None of those compared to the gala atmosphere this evening. Since the governor and other high-ranking officials would be in attendance, the media was out in force, and there were plenty of uniformed cops, probably some guys he knew from when he worked in Cheyenne.

As he scanned faces, looking for someone familiar, he realized that the cops were looking past him, keeping an eye out for threats and troublemakers. He wasn't one of them anymore, and it made him sad. He'd been a good cop, an honest cop. It was a decent job.

A red carpet covered the front entryway, and there were designated places for arriving guests to stand, be photographed and talk to people with microphones.

Jake was privileged to be escorting three beautiful women: Callie, Maggie and the princess. Callie emerged from the limo with a great deal of poise. Her gown was conservative. Her manner, low-key. She was representing the Secretary of Foreign Affairs and needed to present a statesmanlike image. In contrast, Maggie bubbled over with excitement. In the gown she'd borrowed from Saida, she was as fresh and pretty as a new peach. He wasn't sure what she'd done with her makeup, but her lopsided grin seemed sophisticated.

Then Saida stepped onto the carpet. Though she'd told him that the stone in her necklace wasn't a precious gem but a green crystal from Namibia, it sparkled like a million bucks. She'd also explained that jewels in her upswept hair weren't a crown but a re-purposed necklace with white crystals surrounding green ovals. Her gown—which she referred to as "definitely last season"—was simple but perfectly fitted to her tiny waist. In his opinion, she was every inch a princess.

The cameras were drawn to her. Moths to a flame, they swarmed. But they didn't come too close. She seemed to radiate a royal force field that held them at a distance, as though she was a flame and coming too close meant getting burned.

As he accompanied the ladies, Jake heard his own name being mentioned. It seemed strange that he'd be noticed, but then he remembered the real reason he was here. The attorney general, a man who he'd met only once before, wanted him to let everybody know that things hadn't gotten out of hand in Wind River County.

Every time a microphone got stuck in his face, he offered a variation on that theme: *We're all cooperating. Everything is under control. We should be wrapping up our investigation any day now.*

He recognized the woman reporter with bright red lipstick; she had to be the Lipstick Lady blogger who had embarrassed Saida. He couldn't let her libelous comments pass. He crossed the carpet and stood before her.

"Put down that microphone for a minute," he said. "I want to talk to you off the record."

She flashed a grin. "Whatever you say, Wolfman."

"You do the Lipstick Lady blog, right?"

"Right. Have you read my work?"

"I have," he said, "and I'd advise you to check your facts before you write. Nobody likes a bully."

Her bravado crumpled. "It's my job to be outrageous."

"You can do your job without hurting anybody."

He turned his back, but she grasped his arm. Her voice was hostile. "So, is it safe for me to say that you and the princess are hooking up?"

"If we were, and I'm not saying we are, it would be something good and special. And private."

"Oh, my God." She gasped. "You're sexy and sensitive."

Saida appeared beside him. "Back off, Lipstick."

"Princess." The microphone was back. "Do you have a comment?"

Saida looked up at him. "I believe Sheriff Wolf has said it all."

She took his arm and moved toward the entrance. "Did you mean that? About you and me being special?"

"I don't say things I don't mean."

When they finally got inside the ballroom, he encountered about three minutes of calm—enough time to notice the chandeliers, the glow of an ice sculpture and the clink of champagne glasses. There was a dance band and a few couples were gliding across the floor.

Maggie popped up beside him, beaming. "This is awesome."

Her lipstick was already gone, and a chunk of hair had come loose from the up-do. He thought she was adorable. "You're awesome."

She opened her tiny purse to show him her cell phone. "Do you think it's okay if I take pictures? I've never seen an ice sculpture of a Brahma bull. And I think I spotted that movie star who has a ranch in the Tetons."

"Pictures are fine," Saida answered, "as long as you don't sell them to the tabloids."

Jake's momentary respite ended when Saida directed him toward a group of men in tuxedos. "Oil company executives," she explained. "It's time for me to work the room."

"Being here is a job for you," he said.

"Of course. I'm the ambassador for Jamala." Her smile faltered at the edges. "I wish Amir could be here."

"Your brother would be proud of you."

She reached up and patted his cheek. "Lipstick was right. You're sexy and sensitive."

"And I'm carrying a gun."

As the evening wore on, they drifted into different groups. He was consumed by a crowd of politicians and higher-ups in the law enforcement community. Many of them he'd met before and they'd barely taken notice. Now, they were all over him. The media coverage of the COIN crimes had gotten national attention, and people wanted to make sure that he wouldn't make Wyoming look like a primitive backwater.

He talked to the head of the FBI in Cheyenne, the state attorney general, a senator and a state representative. He met the governor and his wife.

Finding Oscar and his wife was a definite relief. Saida joined them and did a fist bump with Mrs. Oscar before they settled into girl talk about their respective jewelry.

Oscar pulled him aside. In a low voice, he said, "I like this princess of yours."

"She's not mine." *Not yet, anyway.*

"Did you notice that Virginia Maddox is here?"

Jake had recognized Big Burt's wife. A small, mousey woman who he knew to have a sharp tongue, maybe she was more shrew than mouse. "She's not real fond of me. I doubt she'll even say hello."

"That's when you send in the princess," Oscar said. "In case you hadn't noticed, every man in the room wants her and every woman wants to be her friend."

That sounded like a plan to him. But before he went back to investigating, he had a different idea. How many times in his life would he be at a ball? "Let's take our ladies and dance."

The band was playing a slow tune with a waltz beat that suited Jake very well. He knew how to dance. Growing up with three sisters, he'd been recruited to act as their partner at an early age. Confidently, he took Saida's hand and led her to the floor.

As he held her, she tilted her head and gazed up at him. Her caramel eyes slanted like an exotic cat, no doubt a trick of makeup. And her knowing smile was suggestive enough that his mind conjured up the possibilities of what might happen after they left the ball. They had adjoining rooms at the hotel. Maggie would be going home with Oscar and his wife. Callie had informed him that she'd be staying with someone else in town.

Her body pressed lightly against his. He took the lead, and she followed so gracefully that her feet didn't seem to touch the floor. The music buoyed them. They were dancing on a cloud in their own private world.

"You're good," she said.

"Surprised?"

"Not really. A lot of athletes are good dancers."

He hadn't thought of himself as an athlete in years. "The Lakers?"

"Terrible dancers," she said. "They're too tall."

He swept her in a twirl that flared her skirt. This should have been an opportunity for him to talk to her about Virginia Maddox, but he couldn't think of anything but Saida. She filled his senses until he was overwhelmed.

When the song ended, they politely clapped. She asked, "What were you and Oscar talking about?"

"Virginia Maddox. Oscar thinks she has a connection with

Dormund." He gave her a thumbnail sketch of Virginia wanting to divorce Big Burt and using Dormund to investigate her husband. "Virginia won't talk to me."

"I'll take care of it," she promised.

Given his druthers, Jake would have spent the rest of the night with her, dancing and standing close enough to smell the fragrance of her perfume. He would have been content to simply stand and stare dumbly at her.

One of the oil execs she'd been talking to earlier approached and asked her to dance. She twirled away in the arms of another man. Saida was in her element, the belle of the ball. This was a world she occupied gracefully, a world that was uncomfortable for him.

In the later part of the evening, he found himself talking basketball with one of the senators and a rancher from Casper. The senator suggested that Jake might consider running for office, and the rancher agreed. "It'd be good to have an Indian in politics, but I don't know if you can really represent all the people of our fair state."

The senator corrected, "You ought to say Native American. Is that right, Jake? Is that what you like to be called?"

The tinge of prejudice was subtle but apparent. He could have told them that he was born Arapaho and grew up on the rez, that he went to University of Wyoming and worked as a cop in Cheyenne. His life was about more than where he was born. "You can call me sheriff. Excuse me, gentlemen."

He saw that Maggie was getting ready to leave with Oscar and made sure that she was safely on her way. Callie had already departed.

That left the princess. Extricating Saida from the grasp of investors and execs wasn't easy. At first, she'd charmed these men with her beauty. Now, she was talking business.

He could see the benefit of the hours she'd spent with the COIN princes. Her comments were intelligent and educated.

He grinned to himself. *That's right, boys. She's more than a pretty face.*

Saida was the whole package, and she made her departure gracefully and politely. Finally, they headed out the side door to the limo.

Sprawled in the backseat, he exhaled in a whoosh and pretended to mop his brow. "That was work."

"I can't wait until Amir is back. He should be having these conversations."

"You did good. The boys from COIN were smart to use you to make these contacts. You're like a secret weapon."

"That's me. The stealth bombshell from Jamala." She scooted across the seat until she was right beside him. "And what about you? I kept hearing your name being whispered."

"If I don't get things cleared up in Wind River County, you'll hear my name, all right. All those people will be calling for my head."

"Which reminds me," she said. "Virginia Maddox."

He wasn't anxious to get back to the investigation, but it couldn't be helped. "Did she know Dormund?"

"Mostly she talked about how her husband had tons of assets and accounts that are completely hidden. Before she divorces him, she's got to find the money."

She leaned her head against his shoulder and adjusted his arm to wrap around her shoulder. They fit together so nicely, so neatly that he wanted to just hold her.

With reluctance, he asked, "Was Dormund the private investigator who was digging into Big Burt's accounts?"

"She didn't hire him directly. He's on retainer for the firm that's handling her divorce. She spoke to Dormund on the phone. They talked about race horses."

"Did he find the hidden accounts?"

"According to Virginia, Dormund was a total failure."

There must have been a reason Oscar pointed him in this

direction. Jake flipped the situation upside down and took another look. "Maybe Dormund was a total success. Maybe he located some of the places Big Burt has been hiding his money."

"Race horses," she said. "Raising and breeding those animals can be a money pit, especially if they lose."

Jake knew that Maddox had taken in a lot of money in bribes when he was sheriff, but no one had been able to prove impropriety. He could have masked his cash flow in race horse investments. "If Dormund contacted Big Burt and told him what he'd discovered, that would be a motive for murder."

"It doesn't make sense," she said. "That motive has nothing to do with the COIN nations, and it doesn't explain why Dormund tried to kidnap me."

"But it's something to consider."

She swiveled around in the seat so she was facing him. Her slender hand caressed his cheek. "There's something else I'm considering."

He turned his head and kissed her hand. "So am I."

"It has nothing to do with COIN or the ball or even the investigation." Her eyes teased. "It's about you, Jake."

"I think we're on the same page."

He glanced through the window. Couldn't this limo go any faster?

Chapter Twenty-Two

At their hotel, Saida and Jake stood in the hallway outside their separate rooms. She inserted her key card in the lock, and pushed the door open. They hadn't discussed the sleeping arrangements, but—as he had said—they were on the same page. Tonight, they would share a bed.

In her room, she found the dress Maggie had worn, neatly draped over a chair. The jeweled shoes were tucked beneath it. On the dresser was a note that read "Thank you, dear Saida, for tonight. I felt like a princess. Maggie."

Saida was touched. Maggie was like the younger sister she'd never had. No matter what happened between her and Jake, she'd stay in contact with this woman.

But not tonight. Saida was extremely glad that Jake's sister was staying with Oscar and his family instead of here at the hotel. Callie had also made other plans. The room was free. The rest of the night belonged to her and Jake.

Kicking off her high heels, she crossed the carpet to one of the queen-size beds and pulled back the tan-and-ivory patterned spread. These linens weren't as luxurious as those at the Wind River Resort, not that it mattered. She didn't require a five-star hotel room. Still, she wanted everything to be perfect for Jake. She might even call room service and order fresh strawberries and chocolate.

She heard him tap on the door to their adjoining room, and

she dashed toward it. Her palm rested on the door, anxious to throw it open. At the same time, she had preparations. "I'm not ready."

"I don't mind."

She had plans for what would happen. In her suitcase was a magnificent silk and lace negligee in a mysterious midnight-blue. "Be patient."

"Why?"

"I need to wash my face and comb my hair and change out of this gown." She'd like to take a bath and use that scented oil that made her skin feel so soft. And there really should be music. "You'll simply have to wait."

"Nope," he said. "Can't do it."

"Jake, don't be silly."

"Saida, don't make me shoot the lock off this door."

"You wouldn't." *Would he?*

"Probably not. I could pick this lock."

"All right." She unfastened her side of the lock and stepped back.

Through the open doors, they stood, staring at each other. Two people from opposite sides of the world with very different lives, they never should have met, never should have had anything in common. But she knew that this tall, dark man was her destiny.

He crossed the threshold into her room and pulled her into an embrace. His kiss was hard and demanding, and she forgot all the lovely preparations she had intended. There was no need for fancy nightgowns and strawberries to fuel their passion. From the first moment they met, she knew that Jake was immune to flirting.

He saw what he wanted and he took it. Right now, he wanted her. And she was willing. She pressed so tightly against him that she couldn't breathe. It didn't matter. She didn't need air. Only him, his touch.

His caresses stroked the length of her body from her shoulder to her bottom. He trailed kisses down her throat toward her breasts. His hands slid down her thighs. He stopped. Suddenly. "What's this?"

Breathing hard, she separated from him. "I told you I needed to get changed."

"What are you wearing?"

Pulling up the long skirt of her gown, she showed him a fitted sheath with a six-inch blade. "You didn't expect me to go to the ball unarmed, did you?"

"It's sexy. Do you have any other weapons?"

"I couldn't wear my gun. It would have ruined the line of my dress." Though she was dizzy with passion, she forced herself to step away from him. "If you don't mind, I'd like to change into something more comfortable."

"Princess, you don't need clothes."

"Nor do you."

"No problem." He threw off his jacket.

"Shirtless," she murmured. That was the way she liked him. Quickly, she unbuttoned his shirt and tugged the sleeves from his shoulders. She loved his lean, muscular chest. His flesh was warm and beautiful.

He caught hold of her hands. His gaze swept the hotel room. "Come to my room."

"Why?"

"For one thing, you've got a lot of girly stuff in here. For another, my bed is bigger."

She was convinced. Taking his hand, she went into his room where the king-size bed awaited.

He unzipped her dress. The fabric fell and puddled on the floor. The lace of her strapless bra squeezed against her taut nipples, and she was relieved to be free from that constraint. She wore only her panties, her necklace and her makeshift tiara.

Before she knew what was happening, he'd lifted her off her feet and carried her to the bed. In a move that would have been appropriate if they'd both been circus acrobats, he lowered her onto the sheets and dropped beside her. In an instant, he tore off his trousers and his howling wolf belt buckle.

His naked flesh pressed against hers. His legs tangled with hers. His fingers caught in her hair. He slowed the pace of their lovemaking, teasing her with fiery caresses and kisses until she couldn't stand it anymore.

"Now, Jake."

"Is that a royal command?"

"When I'm with you, I'm not a princess. Just a woman."

He groped for the bedside table and showed her a stack of condoms. This time, he'd come prepared. And she was ready for him.

THEY SPENT THE NIGHT making love and sleeping in each other's arms. Saida couldn't remember a time when she'd been so happy, excited and content. Being with Jake fulfilled her on levels she didn't know she had.

In the morning, they had to rush to make it to their private jet by eight o'clock. She couldn't believe she'd gotten ready in ten minutes. She'd had plans for breakfast, wanted to treat him with Vietnamese coffee and croissants. Such planning, she realized, was subject to change when she was with Jake. He was the most spontaneous man she'd ever known.

As they fastened their seat belts for takeoff, she said, "You surprise me. You seem to be so methodical, but that's not really you."

"It's not?"

"You're wild." As wild and untamed as the wind in the rugged mountains, he was a force of nature.

"Not usually," he said. "There's something about you that lights my fuse."

When she first looked him up on the internet, she never thought they'd be so good together, so very complementary. It just might be possible for their two worlds to unite.

But probably not. She sighed, reluctantly returning to reality. She hadn't come to Wyoming to meet the man of her dreams. There was something more important. "When we find Amir, everything will be good."

"We'll find your brother."

He'd made that promise before, and she clung to it. If Jake said he was going to do something, he did it. She had to believe that he would bring Amir back to her.

During their flight, they had coffee and sweet rolls. She went into the bathroom to apply makeup but left the door open. "I still haven't reached Granger at that phone number."

"I know." He stood in the doorway, watching her. As she touched her lashes with mascara, he said, "You don't need that stuff. You're beautiful without it."

"Makeup makes me feel put-together. I wouldn't want to face the princes without my best face."

"Like war paint," he said. "Before my tribe went into battle, they painted their faces and bodies. It was supposed to intimidate their enemies."

She liked his analogy. "Makeup is exactly like that."

Before she put on her lipstick, Jake caught her arm. "A kiss first."

It really wasn't smart to start down this path. "We don't have much time before we land."

"Just a kiss."

When his lips met hers, she wanted more. It was impossible to keep her hands off him. She pushed him through the doorway into the narrow hall and pinned him against the wall.

His hand crept inside her shirt. His fingers were cold, and she shivered against him. In an instant, his body warmed. They melted into each other.

When they separated, her senses were swirling like a cyclone. She needed more of him, but there wasn't time. Somehow, she had to make their relationship last for more than a few days.

When they disembarked at the private airfield, Jake unloaded her luggage and his gym bag and carried them to the police SUV he'd left here overnight. She took her cell phone from her purse. From memory, she dialed the mystery number and listened to it ring.

And then, an answer.

A gruff voice demanded, "Who's this?"

"Saida." Finally reaching someone shocked her. She waved frantically to Jake, signaling him. "Who is this?"

"That's for me to know and you to find out."

The childish response made her angry. Of course, it was Granger. Everything pointed to him. Curbing her temper, she asked, "Why did you want me to call you?"

"I know stuff. If you pay me a hundred thousand dollars, I'll tell you everything."

"What do you know?"

"Not so fast, lady. If I tell you, you won't pay me."

This pathetic attempt at extortion was one step up from a crank phone call. He knew "stuff" but wouldn't say what. She felt like throwing the cell phone.

As Jake came toward her, she remembered his advice about how criminals are liars. "How will I know you're telling me the truth? Can you give me a hint?"

"It's about Dormund," he said. "Can you get me the money?"

Jake stood beside her. She repeated Granger's statement so he could hear. "You want one hundred thousand, correct?"

"In small denominations."

Jake signaled her to stall and she said, "It'll take some time to raise that much cash."

"I don't have time. Get as much as you can."

"What if I can't get as much as you want?"

"I'll take anything. Just do it."

He sounded desperate and disorganized. She couldn't rationally negotiate with someone who acted like a five-year-old. "I'll do exactly as you say. I'm very interested in your information."

"Damn right, you are. Damn right."

"Please tell me one thing. Is my brother okay?"

"Who?"

"Sheik Amir Khalid, my brother."

"Lady, I don't know nothing about a sheik."

Her spirits sank. Granger's information wouldn't point her toward Amir. He had some small secret that he thought was worth something. A hundred thousand dollars? Not likely.

She tried to get him talking. "How did you obtain this information about Dormund? Did you kill him?"

"I never did." His voice rose to a level near panic. "I never did nothing wrong. Okay, maybe I banged your car around with my truck, but you didn't get hurt."

"Do you know the killer?"

"That's what I'm trying to tell you. Damn it, pay attention. I know who killed him, shot him dead. And if you pay me, I'll tell you."

"Fine. I'll go to the bank," she said. "And how should we make the exchange? My money for your information."

"Don't you worry," he said. "You get the money, and I'll find you."

He disconnected the call.

She looked up at Jake and shook her head. "Worthless."

"You said something about a hundred thousand dollars."

"That was his demand. He's a very frightened, very stupid man who wants to sell me the name of Dormund's killer."

In Granger's mind, it made some kind of sense to approach her. "Why would he contact me?"

"It's obvious," Jake said. "You've got money."

Of course, she cared about finding the murderer. But her focus was Amir. It had always been Amir. She needed to find her brother. "Granger wants me to go to the bank. He's foolish enough to think that I can stroll through the door and come away with a hundred thousand."

"How does he want to make the exchange?"

"He said that he'd find me."

"I don't like it." Jake took her arm and directed her toward the SUV. "That means he's going to be watching you. It might be smart to put you somewhere you can't be reached."

She wasn't afraid of Granger. "He won't try anything. He sounded desperate, scared as a little kid."

"Which makes him dangerous," he said. "I'm not leaving you alone today. Not for a minute."

That sounded good to her. Maybe she ought to send Granger a thank-you note.

Chapter Twenty-Three

At the bank in downtown Dumont, Saida went into the office of the manager to talk about a wire transfer while Jake called his office. He wasn't anxious to get back to work where a rising tide of details threatened to drown him. The night he'd spent with the princess had been a respite. Those hours of greedy pleasure left him craving more time off, more time with her.

Without trying, she was teaching him how to enjoy life. He hadn't always been super-responsible, putting everybody else's needs ahead of his own. But it had been a long time since he'd allowed himself to relax. Saida showed him how; she made him think it was possible to share his life. With her? Could he spend days, weeks and months with her? It was too much to hope for.

Wheeler came on the phone, and they talked about the case. The forensic report on the crashed rental car came up with fingerprints for Granger and Dormund and other people unrelated to the crimes. It also confirmed his initial analysis that the car had been pushed over the edge of the cliff. Ballistics tests showed that Saida's gun was, in fact, the murder weapon.

Details, details. He wanted to ignore them all, to gather up the princess and ride off with her into a glorious sunset.

Instead, he contacted the FBI agent in charge of the case.

This call was about finances; the feds were better equipped to track down a money trail. If Dormund had been able to find how Maddox was hiding his ill-gotten gains, the FBI ought to be able to do the same.

Jake asked the agent to check out possible money laundering through a race horse scam.

"For Burt Maddox," the agent said. "Sheriff, does this have anything to do with a personal vendetta?"

"Maddox and I don't get along." No secret there. "But this is related to the murder of William Dormund, which is related to the crimes connected to COIN."

"I had to ask."

Jake understood. Maddox had used their personal animosity to dismiss anything negative that Jake said about him, even if it was the truth.

Saida came out of the bank manager's office carrying a small green backpack. Though concern about her brother was never far from her mind, her step had a bounce, and excitement crackled around her.

As they left the bank and stepped onto the sidewalk, she told him that she had a wire transfer for eight thousand dollars. "The bank manager gave me cash and found this pack for me to carry it. This ought to be enough to convince Granger to tell us everything he knows."

"How did you come up with that number?"

"It happened to be the amount in one of my accounts." She glanced along the street at the storefronts. "That's a café on the corner. Maybe we should have brunch."

He seriously doubted that the diner had a brunch menu, but they did serve breakfast twenty-four hours a day. "I could eat."

She held the backpack toward him. "Do you mind carrying it? The green doesn't go with my outfit."

Today, she was dressed in the California version of

Western with boots, tight jeans and an orange drape kind of shirt with a snakeskin belt. They'd only gone about halfway down the block when she came to a halt in front of a small shop with a quilt display in the window. "Is this where the lady we saw in Danny's photos works?"

"I believe it is. Harriet's Quilts."

The inside of the shop was cool, softly lit and cozy. An array of handmade quilts hung from racks and there was a wall of yarn, thread and fancy little detailing. Harriet sat on a stool behind a counter. Her white hair was piled on top of her head in a bun and she was hand-sewing.

Looking up, she pushed her wire-frame glasses up on her nose. When she spied the princess, she let out a little cry of excitement. "Oh, I was hoping you'd come."

Saida moved toward her. "These quilts are lovely. Are they all handmade?"

"You betcha." Harried hopped down from the stool and bustled toward them. "You're even prettier up close, Princess Saida. I've seen all those pictures in the tabloids, but I don't believe any of those terrible things they say about you. I can tell by looking that you're a good girl. Hi, Sheriff."

"Ma'am." He nodded. "You seem to have a real interest in the COIN princes."

"That's right. Especially Jamala." She returned to her counter, bent down and reached underneath. "As soon as I knew about people from Jamala coming here, I went digging through my stock in the back of the shop. Come over here, Princess. There's something I want you to see."

Harriet spread a three-foot by four-foot wall hanging on the counter. The border was red, black and yellow. In the center was a stylized representation of three horses at full gallop. The lead horse was predominantly made from a red-and-gold fabric.

Saida ran her hands across the wall hanging. "Where did you get this material?"

"You recognize it." Harriet's mouth pinched in a smug little bow. "I thought you might."

"This red is from Jamala. It's shot through with copper. I've never seen it anywhere else in the world. And the three horses are our national symbol."

Harriet perched on her stool again. "It was a long time ago, thirty-three years or so, when a handsome young stranger came to town. He had dark hair and dark eyes. Oh, my, he loved to go horseback riding, and he cut a fine figure in the saddle."

"What was his name?" Jake asked.

"He said we should just call him Sundance, like the Sundance Kid." She chuckled. "Of course, that wasn't his real name. He said he was from a place far away. I'm not sure when I heard of Jamala. He didn't talk about it, said he wanted Wyoming to be his home."

"Like Amir," Saida said softly.

"Anyway," she continued, "I was just getting started with making quilts back then, and he saw me sewing and gave me a beautiful, long scarf with this red fabric. It was the sweetest gesture. I was having a kind of rough time. My husband was off in the Marines, and I was working at the Freeman Ranch."

"Freeman," Jake said. "The cattle ranch that's owned by Wade Freeman?"

"Sure enough. Wade wasn't even born until a year later. His mom was kind of sweet on Mr. Sundance. If he'd stayed around a bit longer, she might have gotten hitched to him. The woman was dying to get married. After Sundance left, she moved to Denver for a couple of years, got married and divorced and came back to the ranch with little Wade."

Saida circled the counter and wrapped Harriet in a warm embrace. "Thank you."

"Well, that's all right, dear. I thought you might be acquainted with that gentleman who came here so many years ago."

"I might know him." Saida picked up the wall hanging. "Would you consider selling this piece?"

"Certainly. It ought to go home with you."

Saida unzipped the backpack, reached inside and pulled out several banded stacks of twenties. The amount had to be over a thousand dollars. "Thank you again, Harriet. I'll be back to visit with you."

OUTSIDE THE QUILT SHOP, Saida announced what they must do. "We have to go to the Freeman Ranch. I've got to talk to Wade Freeman."

Jake didn't object, even though he had a million other things he should be doing. He understood how important this revelation was.

Why hadn't Amir told her? When he came to Wyoming last year to see Freeman, it wasn't to discuss the price of oil. Amir had been following a path that was blazed by their father some thirty-three years ago. Calling himself Sundance, their father had sown his wild oats at the Freeman Ranch, after which Wade's mother had disappeared for a time, and then returned with a child.

To Saida, it was obvious what had happened. Her father had sired a son while he was in Wyoming. She shouldn't have been surprised. Her father was a notorious womanizer. The real shocker should have been that he hadn't left illegitimate children all over the globe.

She climbed into the passenger seat of Jake's SUV and fastened her seat belt. "I wouldn't have believed a word that Harriet said if I hadn't seen that cloth from Jamala."

"The red fabric?"

"I have a scarf with me that's made from the same fabric."

"I remember," he said. "Maggie liked it."

As he pulled away from the curb, she turned toward him, grateful that he was steady and strong. She needed his stability to keep herself grounded. "Am I overreacting?"

"To the possibility that Wade Freeman is your long lost half brother?" He reached across the console, took her hand and squeezed. "It's all right for you to go a little bit crazy. That's a big pill to swallow."

"Why didn't my father tell us? We should have known that we had an American half brother. If Harriet has the timing right, it means that my father came here and had his fling with Wade's mother right before he settled into marriage with my mother."

The full weight of what she'd said hit her like an anvil. "Amir is thirty-one. Wade is older. That means Wade Freeman is the rightful sheik of Jamala."

"Technically, he's a bastard son," Jake said. "Does that make a difference?"

"In the old days, it would have. If Wade showed up to claim his rightful place, he would have been seen as a pretender. Now, we have DNA testing to prove his heritage."

She rested her hand on her breast and felt her heart thumping. She wished that Nasim was here to counsel her. How should she handle the situation? Should she denounce Wade Freeman? But he was her blood relation. Other than Amir, she had no one else.

"Here's what worries me," Jake said. "Wade Freeman has a claim to becoming ruler of your country. That gives him a real good reason to want Amir out of the way."

She sank back in the seat and stared blankly through the windshield. Jake was absolutely right. No one had a better motive than Wade Freeman for wanting Amir to disappear.

He could have been thinking about this for years, could have been plotting his revenge. She recalled, "He said that his mother died about a year ago. He must have been waiting for her death to make his move."

"I don't see him as a villain," Jake said. "Freeman is a rancher, and he seems pretty happy with his lifestyle."

She turned on him. "You can't possibly understand the greed and the intrigues of royal conspiracies. You never know who you can trust and who is going to betray you. You have to watch every word."

"You're right. Your life as a princess is something I don't understand."

A gulf opened between them. For the first time since she met Jake, she felt distant from him. "I tried to reject that life by moving to America."

"You can't change who you are."

He stared straight ahead with his hands on the steering wheel. She wished he would turn to her and smile, wished that he would assure her that everything was all right between them. She wanted to tell him that she'd cast off her title in a minute to be with him. But she couldn't.

No matter how hard she tried, she couldn't escape her heritage.

Chapter Twenty-Four

At the Freeman Ranch, Jake was told by the ranch foreman that Wade Freeman was repairing fences in the south field where a good portion of the herd was grazing. Jake wouldn't have minded hanging around and drinking coffee until Wade returned to the ranch house, but Saida's anxiety was sky-high. She was so agitated that she could barely stand still. Waiting was out of the question.

The only way to reach the south field was by using an all-terrain vehicle or by horseback. Since all the ATVs were in use, the foreman got them saddled up and pointed in the right direction. From his knowledge of local landmarks, Jake had a good idea of where they needed to go. Locating four hundred head of cattle shouldn't be difficult.

He glanced over at Saida as she rode beside him. They'd hit an impasse in their relationship. The differences between them had never seemed so insurmountable.

She adjusted the strap on the shoulder bag where she carried her Beretta. She'd said that they needed to keep the backpack with them. It seemed unnecessary, but he didn't argue. Instead, he'd slipped the backpack on. One more frustration might send her over the edge into a royal nervous breakdown.

At the top of a hill at the edge of a forest, she reined her horse. "What am I going to say to Freeman?"

"You're good at negotiations. You'll figure it out."

She shook her head, and her hair fell forward to hide her face. "I'm scared. All I can think of are the negatives. What if Freeman has already killed Amir and buried his body? We'll never find him."

Her words sent a chill through him. It was the first time she'd acknowledged that Amir might be dead. He couldn't let her give up hope. "I made you a promise, Saida. I said that I'd find your brother, and I will."

He heard the sound of an ATV motor. Nothing unusual about that. Every ranch used these raucous four-wheel machines that were cheaper to maintain than horses. But he sensed danger approaching. He drew his weapon and held it at his side.

The ATV came closer. Jake squinted into the sun, trying to recognize the rider. He raised his gun. "Granger."

Beside him, Saida started. "What?"

"It's Granger. He must have been following us, tracking us." Jake was actually impressed by Granger's ability to follow them without being seen. "He's a good hunter. And sneaky as hell."

"But not very bright," she said. "He's got to know that you're going to arrest him."

Granger parked, turned off the ATV and climbed off it. He looked like he'd been sleeping in the forest and living off tree bark. "Give me the money," he demanded.

"Don't move." Jake aimed at the center of Granger's skinny chest. "I'll shoot."

Granger spread his arms wide. "Everybody wants to kill me. Might as well get it over with."

"That's enough," Saida snapped. "Mr. Granger, you said you had information for me. I wish to hear it."

His eyes shifted from side to side. "If I tell you, will the sheriff let me go?"

"Tell me," she said imperiously. "And we'll see if we can come to an arrangement."

"Damn it all, things weren't supposed to turn out like this. I was meaning to do the right thing. I was going to tell the lady and get some money, and then I figured she'd tell you, Sheriff."

"Start talking," Jake said.

"You going to arrest me? If you do, I'm as good as dead. Maddox will have me killed in jail, just like Amos Andrews."

Andrews was a dirty cop who supposedly committed suicide while he was in custody. Jake had suspected murder but couldn't prove it. "What do you know about Andrews?"

"I know a hell of a lot." Granger sounded proud of himself. "You'd be smart to take me into protective custody. You know, like those witness protection programs. I could start a new life."

"Tell me about Dormund's murder," Jake said.

"Maddox paid Dormund big bucks to keep him quiet about some race horse scam. Dormund was on the payroll. Maddox had him come here and get a rental car." He glanced toward Saida. "We were fixing to kidnap the lady."

"Why?" Jake asked.

"It didn't have nothing to do with her." Granger showed his yellow teeth in a sick grin. "It was all about you, Sheriff. Maddox figured if we kidnapped her, you'd look real bad. Everybody'd know that you can't handle Big Burt's job."

The attempted abduction was nothing but a ploy. Maddox intended to use the COIN crimes—the explosions, the snipers, the traitors—to destroy him. "None of this is connected to Amir's disappearance."

"Hell, no. I don't know where he's gone off to. And I don't give a crap."

"You still haven't told me who murdered Dormund."

Granger held out a filthy hand. "And you haven't given

me my money. Even if I'm a protected witness, I'm going to need some cash. Ain't that right?"

He really was an idiot. There was no point in explaining reality to him. Jake tossed the backpack on the ground near Granger's feet. "Tell me what you saw?"

He scrambled to pick up the pack and unzipped it. He clutched a handful of cash in his fist. "Hey, this isn't enough."

"There's more where that came from," Saida said. "Talk."

"Maddox shot Dormund in the rental car, then we moved him to my truck. And we left that pretty little earring to hook things up with the lady. The way Maddox figured, Dormund's murder would get lumped in with all the other royal crimes. Nobody would come looking for him."

Jake wanted to believe that he might ultimately have discovered the truth, but he had to give Maddox credit. If Granger had disappeared, there was a good likelihood that Dormund's murder would have gone unsolved.

"Why are you telling me this?" Jake asked.

"Maddox already got away with murder. Twice, if you count Amos Andrews. It wouldn't be long before he came after me."

"Has he threatened you?"

"I've been hiding out ever since you found my truck. That's why I didn't answer my phone."

"You were scared," Jake said.

Granger's jaw tensed. No man liked to admit he was frightened. "Maybe."

Three gunshots exploded.

Granger was shot in the chest. He threw up his hands, tossing the money into the air. His legs crumpled and he fell to the ground.

Maddox and two of his men rode out of the nearby trees. They were all armed. The two men aimed their rifles at Jake and Saida. She was positioned between him and Maddox. Her eyes were frantic. "What should I do?"

"Don't move. Not yet."

Maddox rode closer. "Drop your gun, Jake. Do it now or I'll have them kill her."

If he discarded his weapon, Jake would have no way to defend himself. Maddox couldn't let them live. Not with what they knew.

His only chance was to stall. He knew they were close enough to the south field for Freeman and his men to have heard the gunshots. He had to hope that they'd come to investigate.

"Finally," Jake said. "Finally, I get to see your true colors, Maddox."

"Drop it. I'm not joking."

Jake didn't have a choice. He dropped his gun where he could reach it easily if he dismounted. He called out to the two men flanking Maddox. "Let me ask you boys. You think he's going to let you live? Or do you think you're going to end up like poor old Granger."

"My men are loyal," Maddox said. "Granger was a rat."

Jake focused on the other two men. "You don't want to do this. Killing a sheriff will get you in serious trouble."

"A sheriff," Maddox said with a sneer.

Jake deliberately provoked him. "I beat you, fair and square."

"You're nothing but a damn, dirty Indian. We never should have let your people off the reservation."

"Is that so? Well, let me tell you what happened at the Cattlemen's Ball in Cheyenne. The governor wants me to run for the senate. By the way, Virginia says hello."

"That bitch."

"She's the one who got you into all this trouble, sending Dormund to investigate. Who would have thought he'd be smart enough to figure out how you were hiding your money."

Maddox raised his rifle. "I should shoot you right now."

"But not me." When Saida spoke, her voice was steady. "I have a great deal of influence and money. I'd be happy to pay you gentlemen four times what you're earning right now."

She turned her shoulder bag around as though she would reach inside and pull out a fresh stack of cash. Jake knew what she intended. She meant to take out her own gun. But then, she'd become the target. He couldn't let that happen.

"Let's wait a second, Princess."

She looked toward him, and he subtly shook his head.

"Don't bother," Maddox said. "My men aren't going to fall for her lies. She's a foreigner. Her country means to rip off our American oil business."

Jake heard the buzz of approaching ATVs. Freeman and his men were coming to see what the shooting was about. Their vehicles were already in sight.

"Here comes our backup," Jake said. "You can't kill us all."

His men lowered their rifles and exchanged a look. They dug in their heels and rode away fast. Maddox turned in his saddled and yelled after them. "Cowards. Stay here."

Jake took advantage of his momentary distraction. He swung down from his horse, grabbed his gun and aimed at Maddox.

When he glanced toward Saida, he saw that she'd drawn her Beretta. Both of their weapons were trained and steady.

"Burt Maddox," Jake said, "you're under arrest."

As Jake took the former sheriff into custody, Saida dismounted. Her legs were shaky, and her hand trembled. If she'd been required to shoot Maddox, she wasn't sure that she could have pulled the trigger.

Wade Freeman and two other men had arrived on their four-wheelers. Wade ran past Granger, bleeding on the ground, and came to her. "Saida, are you all right? Were you hurt?"

In his dark eyes and firm jaw, she saw a reflection of her brother. She should have guessed at their relationship the moment she'd met him.

Fighting tears, she asked, "Why didn't you tell me?"

"I wanted to. I saw the family resemblance right away, and I wanted to hug you. But I promised Amir that I would wait."

"Why?"

"He didn't want to talk about our relationship until after the COIN summit."

The only reason Amir would have for keeping this huge secret was because he couldn't risk having a challenge to his leadership. "You're the eldest. Do you intend to assert your rights as my father's heir?"

"Never." His voice was deep and sincere. The tone reminded her of Amir. "I never knew who my father was. My mom didn't tell me until she was on her deathbed. Then she talked about a handsome sheik who came to Wyoming and fell in love. She showed me a wooden cigar box, wrapped in a red scarf. Inside were two passionate letters and this." He opened the top button on his shirt. On a chain around his neck, he wore a ring emblazoned with the three-horse crest of Jamala.

"A tragic story."

"Not at all," he said. "When he left, she never expected to see him again. My mom was a Freeman, born and bred to be a cattle rancher. This ranch was her life. Mine, too."

She was beginning to believe that Wade Freeman didn't

mean any harm to her or her brother. "When did you contact Amir?"

"That happened the way I told you. We talked about oil projects. One thing led to another, and then I showed him the ring." He gave her a smile. "How did you find out?"

"Harriet at the quilt shop."

"I wasn't aware that she knew."

"Not only does she know, but she made a wall hanging to commemorate the meeting of your mother and my father. I'd like to give it to you."

"I'd appreciate that. It's taking me a while to get accustomed to the whole idea. I never had brothers or sisters."

"Now you do."

"I hope you won't be offended if I don't change my name to Khalid and move to Jamala. I'm a Freeman. My home is right here on this ranch."

"The name doesn't matter." She threw both arms around his neck. "Welcome to the family, brother."

She clung to him for a long moment.

Jake had been right when he'd said that Freeman was happy in Wyoming and had no designs on becoming the ruler of her country. The main reason her mind had gone down that path was because she'd been spending so much time with the COIN royals. When she was around them, everything seemed like a complicated conspiracy. Life wasn't meant to be so difficult.

She smiled up at her brother. "We'll have a chance to get to know each other. I'll be spending more time in Wyoming."

"Until we find Amir."

"Yes."

She went toward Jake. As usual, he was juggling several responsibilities at the same time. Keeping an eye on Maddox who was being held by Freeman's men. Covering Granger's body to give him the dignity in death that he lacked in life. And talking on his cell phone to Wheeler.

As he ended his call, she took custody of the phone, compelling him to face her. "I wanted to tell you that you were right about Freeman. You've been right about a lot of things."

"I hope," he said, "that I wasn't right about you and me being from such different worlds that we could never—"

"There's only one world, Jake. And it's a world where you and I are together."

In spite of the people watching, he pulled her into his arms and kissed her on the lips. Still holding her, he whispered, "I want you to stay with me."

Her father had come to Wind River County, fallen in love and run away. She wouldn't make the same mistake. "I won't leave you."

"I'm going to find your brother."

Regret cut into her happiness. Though she still felt a connection to Amir, they hadn't come any closer to discovering where he was or what had happened to him. "That might be a promise you can't keep."

"I won't take back my promise, and I won't stop looking. I mean what I say. I don't lie, especially not to the woman I love."

As soon as he spoke the word, she knew it was true. "I love you, too. And I have a promise."

He leaned back so he could look into her eyes. "I'm listening."

"Next season. Opening game. Courtside seats for the Lakers."

He lifted her off the ground and spun her in a circle. "I'm there."

And so was she. There with him, forever.

* * * * *

*COWBOYS ROYALE comes to a
heart-stopping conclusion with
THE BLACK SHEEP SHEIK
by Dana Marten.
Look for it next month wherever
Harlequin Intrigue books are sold!*

INTRIGUE®

COMING NEXT MONTH

Available September 13, 2011

You can find more information on upcoming
Harlequin® titles, free excerpts and more at
www.HarlequinInsideRomance.com.

HICNM0811

New York Times *and* USA TODAY *bestselling author*
Maya Banks presents a brand-new miniseries

PREGNANCY & PASSION

When four irresistible tycoons face
the consequences of temptation.

Book 1—ENTICED BY HIS FORGOTTEN LOVER

Available September 2011 from Harlequin® Desire®!

Rafael de Luca had been in bad situations before. A crowded ballroom could never make him sweat.

These people would never know that he had no memory of any of them.

He surveyed the party with grim tolerance, searching for the source of his unease.

At first his gaze flickered past her, but he yanked his attention back to a woman across the room. Her stare bored holes through him. Unflinching and steady, even when his eyes locked with hers.

Petite, even in heels, she had a creamy olive complexion. A wealth of inky-black curls cascaded over her shoulders and her eyes were equally dark.

She looked at him as if she'd already judged him and found him lacking. He'd never seen her before in his life. Or had he?

He cursed the gaping hole in his memory. He'd been diagnosed with selective amnesia after his accident four months ago. Which seemed like complete and utter bull. No one got amnesia except hysterical women in bad soap operas.

With a smile, he disengaged himself from the group

around him and made his way to the mystery woman.

She wasn't coy. She stared straight at him as he approached, her chin thrust upward in defiance.

"Excuse me, but have we met?" he asked in his smoothest voice.

His gaze moved over the generous swell of her breasts pushed up by the empire waist of her black cocktail dress.

When he glanced back up at her face, he saw fury in her eyes.

"Have we *met?*" Her voice was barely a whisper, but he felt each word like the crack of a whip.

Before he could process her response, she nailed him with a right hook. He stumbled back, holding his nose.

One of his guards stepped between Rafe and the woman, accidentally sending her to one knee. Her hand flew to the folds of her dress.

It was then, as she cupped her belly, that the realization hit him. She was pregnant.

Her eyes flashing, she turned and ran down the marble hallway.

Rafael ran after her. He burst from the hotel lobby, and saw two shoes sparkling in the moonlight, twinkling at him.

He blew out his breath in frustration and then shoved the pair of sparkly, ultrafeminine heels at his head of security.

"Find the woman who wore these shoes."

Will Rafael find his mystery woman?
Find out in Maya Banks's passionate new novel
ENTICED BY HIS FORGOTTEN LOVER
Available September 2011 from Harlequin® Desire®!